ICE CREAM
SUMMER

Don't miss the next Orchard Novel!

ONCE UPON A WINTER

· AN ORCHARD NOVEL ·

ICE CREAM SUMMER

By Megan Atwood

Illustrated by Natalie Andrewson

ALADDIN

New York London Toronto Sydney New Delhi

ALADDIN

An imprint of Simon & Schuster Children's Publishing Division

1230 Avenue of the Americas, New York, New York 10020

First Aladdin hardcover edition May 2017

Text copyright © 2017 by Simon & Schuster, Inc.

Illustrations copyright © 2017 by Natalie Andrewson

All rights reserved, including the right of reproduction in whole or in part in any form.

ALADDIN and related logo are registered trademarks of Simon & Schuster, Inc.

For information about special discounts for bulk purchases, please contact Simon & Schuster Special Sales at 1-866-506-1949 or business@simonandschuster.com.

The Simon & Schuster Speakers Bureau can bring authors to your live event. For more information or to book an event contact the Simon & Schuster Speakers Bureau at 1-866-248-3049 or visit our website at www.simonspeakers.com.

Book designed by Laura Lyn DiSiena

The illustrations for this book were rendered digitally.

The text of this book was set in Baskerville.

Manufactured in the United States of America 0317 FFG

10 9 8 7 6 5 4 3 2 1

This book has been cataloged with the Library of Congress.

ISBN 978-1-4814-9047-4 (hc)

ISBN 978-1-4814-9048-1 (eBook)

To my parents, who are the most amazing parents a person could hope for. I love you both to the moon and back (and I miss you, Mom).

CHAPTER 1

Bubble Gum, Cotton Candy, and Birthday Cake Swirl with a Cherry on Top (But No Whipped Cream Because That's Too Sweet and We're [Mostly] Not Maniacs Here)

Sarah sprinted out of the house, barely slowing down enough to yell, "GOING TO THE GARRISONS'!" at her mom. Her mom always knew anyway. Sarah practically lived at the orchard down the road—after all, her best friend lived there. She hopped on her bike and pedaled hard.

She rode past the long fence that traveled the property. Past the little ice cream stand that ran in the summers. She rode past rows and rows of apple trees, a big red barn, and a big gravel parking lot. As she rode she took a deep breath of the summer air. She loved the smell of the orchard, especially in the summer. But today the ride to Lizzie's house was taking forever. Because today Lizzie and Sarah were going to find out if they would get to run the ice cream stand for the summer. Alone. For the first time.

Sarah rode up the long gravel driveway and then hopped off while her bike was still going. She dropped the bike on the ground, one wheel still spinning, and ran to the wraparound porch, stomping up the wood steps. Lizzie stood just outside the door, bouncing on her toes, her blondish-brown hair bouncing with her. "You're here!" she said. Sarah would have snorted at anyone else. Because, duh. But she'd known Lizzie for so long that she knew that translated to: "You're late." And "You took forever." And "I've been waiting." Lizzie couldn't seem to say words that made other people feel bad.

Sarah held her side and took a deep breath. "Had to . . . shelve . . . books." As the only child of the only librarian in town, she often had to fill in for any missing volunteers. That meant shelving a LOT of books. She didn't even like to read that much. Plus, her mom always had her do the books for babies. The last one she'd shelved was called *I Pottied, Too.*

The screen door opened and Lizzie's mom, Ms. G, breezed out, something sticky on her cheeks and fudge smeared around her mouth. She licked the fudge off and said, "Here you are,

Sarah!" in her booming voice. Around Lizzie's mom, Sarah always felt like she was caught in a whirlwind.

She grinned. "Ms. G, you have marshmallow on your face."

Ms. G grinned back. "One must fully immerse oneself in an experience to truly understand it." She wiped her face with her hand and winked at Sarah.

Lizzie's teenage sister, Gloria, suddenly popped out of the screen door. "ACTING!" she yelled. Then popped back inside. She had probably been walking down the huge staircase inside and heard the word "immerse." Sarah had learned that words like "immerse," or "method," or "feelings," always seemed to make Gloria pop out of nowhere and yell "ACTING!" Evidently, they were words famous actors used. Gloria said they were part of the "craft," whatever that meant. Ever since she had decided to be an actress two years ago, she'd taken the whole thing very seriously.

Most of the time, Sarah had no idea what Gloria was talking about. All she knew was that Gloria had gotten a scholarship to acting camp for a whole month of the summer. Leaving Lizzie and Sarah the most likely candidates to run the stand—the youngest Garrison-and-best-friend duo ever. IF Lizzie's parents agreed. Gloria was three whole years older than Lizzie and Sarah and heading into high school next year. Lizzie and Sarah had to prove to the Garrisons they were just as mature as Gloria. They thought that was a no-brainer.

Ms. G said, "Well, come in, you two! I just have to find that spacey husband of mine and we can give you the g—" She stopped herself and then put on a serious face. "The news, that is. We'll see if it's good or bad."

Sarah shared a look with Lizzie. This was DEFINITELY promising. A zing of excitement shot through Sarah, making her whole body vibrate. Lizzie bounced on her toes again and squeaked.

"Have you seen your father, darling?" Ms. G's hair was now stuck in the marshmallow on her cheek.

Lizzie furrowed her brow. "Last I saw him he was in the backyard, I think. He was kind of just staring up at the gazebo."

Sarah couldn't blame Mr. G. The gazebo

was one of Sarah's favorite places in the whole orchard. She and Lizzie had had their best talks in there.

"Ah," Ms. G said. "All right then. I'll go scare him up and you two go sit in the kitchen, yes? We'll talk about your summer fate." She winked at them and then whirled down the porch steps.

Gloria popped out. "ACTING!" she yelled. Then popped back inside, slamming the screen door.

"How was that . . . ?" Sarah started.

Lizzie shrugged. "I have no idea how that had anything to do with acting. She's just, you know. Creative." Lizzie grabbed Sarah's hand. Her eyes twinkled. "Come on, let's go sit down. Mom has an ice cream bar set up."

Sarah didn't have to be told twice. She

followed Lizzie into the sprawling house with the creaky wood doors and the huge staircase. Lizzie patted the banister three times and Sarah followed suit—they always did that when they came in together. Sarah couldn't remember when they'd started doing it. It was just what you did when you came into the house.

Now Sarah and Lizzie sprinted past the banister and through the sunroom. They rounded the corner to the huge dining room that sat outside the kitchen cutout. The gigantic wood table didn't have its usual centerpiece with wildflowers and a bowl of apples. Instead, at least six types of ice cream from MOO—the ice cream store the Garrisons bought the orchard stand's supply from—sat on the table. Next to the tubs sat sprinkles and caramel, fudge and strawberries, maraschino cherries and whipped cream. Even things like cookie crumbs and candy bar pieces sat there. Sarah's eyes went wide.

Best. Summer. Ever.

Lizzie and Sarah slowed down and circled the table. Sarah knew exactly what Lizzie would want. She'd go for a plain base—vanilla—and then pile different kinds of chocolate on it. After being friends basically since they were babies, Sarah knew everything about Lizzie. She watched and smiled as Lizzie picked up a spoon and headed toward the vanilla.

Sarah grabbed a spoon and was about to scoop some ice cream too—peanut butter swirl, of course—when Mr. and Ms. G walked in, holding hands. They giggled at each other. Sarah thought it was kind of cute but also really gross how much they seemed to love each other. In moments like these, she was glad her mom wasn't with anyone.

Mr. G cleared his throat and pushed up his glasses and said, "Sorry, girls! Just envisioning a glorious new gazebo! Maybe we could turn it into a dance floor—"

Ms. G interrupted. "Maybe next year, dear." Mr. G always had a jazillion ideas for the orchard. But, unfortunately, hardly any of them were realistic. Even Sarah knew that. One time, Mr. G had tried to get her and Lizzie behind the idea of buying a bunch of white horses and gluing unicorn horns to them. Sarah and Lizzie had barely talked him out of it. Ms. G always said, "My honey has million-dollar ideas with zero-dollar follow-through."

Unlike Sarah and Lizzie. Their ideas made sense. Their ideas could even *make* money. Like their favorite idea of all time: a zombie hayride during the fall harvest! But there was never enough money to put one on.

Ms. G said, "Well, girls, why don't you take a seat."

Lizzie and Sarah looked at each other, wide-eyed.

This was it.

They both sat down. Lizzie grabbed Sarah's hand and Sarah squeezed. Her mouth watered at the mingled smells of chocolate, vanilla, and strawberry.

Mr. G grabbed some bowls and set them down, and then he and Ms. G sat across from Lizzie and Sarah. Sarah could hardly breathe.

Mr. G looked at Ms. G and she nodded. They both smiled wide. He said, "I love zombies!" and sat back triumphantly.

Sarah looked at Lizzie. Lizzie looked at her mom. Her mom cleared her throat.

"What your father means, honey"—she patted Mr. G's hand, and he still beamed, but now looked dreamily out the window—"is that we want to offer you and Sarah the positions of ice cream stand operators for the whole summer."

Sarah whooped and Lizzie smiled hugely and clapped her hands. Sarah's mind went wild, thinking of all the things this meant.

First, they could have all the ice cream they wanted.

Second, they had all the power they wanted. Well, that Sarah wanted, anyway. She could give only a few toppings to people she didn't like. Or heap toppings on for people she did. How good an ice cream sundae was depended on the mix of the ingredients—everyone knew that. The wrong amount of an ingredient could ruin a sundae. She had the power to make or break a person's sundae enjoyment. An awesome power.

Third, this meant they would make money all summer. Sarah loved having money. She'd be able to go to all the movies she wanted with Lizzie. Especially the scary ones—her and Lizzie's favorite kind. New Amity didn't have a movie theater, but the bigger town of Hanoverville did.

Fourth, and most important of all: this was a tradition. Gloria and her best friend, Jeff, had run the stand, and Ms. G and her best friend before that. And before that, Lizzie's grand-mother and her best friend. Normally, though, the best friends were fourteen years old—the age they for sure could be trusted with such an important task. So this meant Mr. and Ms. G trusted Sarah and Lizzie with the whole ice cream stand's success, even though they were only eleven.

Ms. G smiled her gigantic smile and said, "But there's more."

Mr. G said, "Honey, have you seen my glasses?"

"They're on your head, dear," she said, then went on. "If you two can make five thousand dollars' profit from the ice cream stand over the summer, we will have enough money to finally run a zombie hayride." Mr. and Ms. G sat back and smiled at the same time.

"WHAT?!" Sarah yelled, jumping to her feet.

Lizzie squealed. "This is . . . ," she started, but then just looked around with a huge smile on her face. Sarah knew she meant "FINALLY WE GET TO DO THIS! I'M SO EXCITED! THIS IS SO COOL!"

Sarah and Lizzie grabbed each other's hands and jumped up and down, whooping, making their chairs squeak across the floor. Sarah felt a tide of relief wash over her, from a worry she didn't ever admit to herself that she had.

The thing was . . . Sarah wasn't *exactly* worried about her and Lizzie's friendship. Not really. Except . . . she'd been noticing lately that they didn't always like the same things anymore. Sarah liked running and sports and math—Lizzie didn't. Lizzie liked reading and drawing and English—Sarah didn't. But a zombie hayride was something they both loved. They'd been talking about it forever. A zombie hayride would just add that one more thing that would make their best-friendship even stronger. The ice cream stand and the zombie hayride together? She and Lizzie would be invincible. Sarah whooped even louder and nearly fell over.

Lizzie's parents laughed at them, but then Ms. G got a serious look on her face. "This means you have to work long hours and have to make sure to get a lot of customers. Otherwise, this won't work. Do you think you can do this? Five thousand dollars is a lot of money."

Lizzie and Sarah looked at each other. Sarah stood up tall. Lizzie did too. They both said, "We can do this."

Sarah set her jaw. Nothing would get in the

way of them making that money and putting on a zombie hayride. Nothing.

Mr. G winked at them, and Ms. G said, "Well then, it's settled."

Sarah hugged Lizzie hard. Just her and her best friend, an ice cream stand, and then a zombie hayride, like they'd always planned.

Best. Summer. Ever.

CHAPTER 2

Double Fudge Whammy with Three
Types of M&M's and Two Mounds of
Whipped Cream. Plus a Dollop of UGH.

T hree more," Sarah said. She looked at Lizzie, who was sticking her tongue out as she drew a cherry on one of the flyers. She had glitter in her eyebrows and on her nose. She gave a thumbs-up and Sarah grinned.

The wood floor she and Lizzie sat on looked like a glitter bomb had exploded. She uncapped the glitter glue pen and drew a heart over the "I" in "ice cream" on her fifteenth flyer. She and Lizzie had spent hours on these flyers. She was pretty sure they were the best flyers the town of New Amity, New Hampshire, would ever see. She blew on the glue to help it dry.

"So," Sarah's mom, Anahita Shirvani, said as she walked into the room, a warm smile on her face. She had glitter on the front of her glasses. Her shoes sparkled. A corner of her eyebrow glinted. When she leaned over to look at their masterpieces, her long black hair had glitter all through it. She hadn't even been in the room since they started. "I do appreciate a good glittering. However, I am wondering when you might be cleaning up?"

Sarah translated this to "You're glittering my library books." Frankly, Sarah thought this made them look better. Maybe it would make people pick up more books.

She put the cap back on the glitter pen. "We have three more to do. Where do you think we can put them up in town?" She crossed her fingers. Her mom wasn't always the best at giving advice.

Her mom's face lit up. "I have just the thing!" She turned on her heel and disappeared.

Sarah groaned. Her mom was definitely grabbing a book. This never ended well. For some reason, her mom could never find the right book for her. She could look at a stranger in the library parking lot and guess what they needed. But with Sarah, she always seemed to be a little off. Her last recommendation had been a book on garden gnomes. Which was fine—garden gnomes were cute. Except

Sarah had asked her what she needed to do to get a basil plant to grow.

Lizzie and Sarah shared a look. Lizzie smiled and looked down, stifling a giggle. Sarah grinned.

Sure enough, her mom returned and put a book down in a puff of glitter.

"Here you go!" Ms. Shirvani flourished her arms, as if it was a gold crown. To her, Sarah thought, every book was a gold crown.

She looked at the title of the book. *Boom or Bust? Early Marketing Techniques of the Frontier.* Sarah raised an eyebrow and Lizzie giggled. "Uh, thanks, Mom," Sarah said. "This is great."

Her mom tried. She always tried. She wanted Sarah to like reading. And Sarah didn't *hate* reading, really. But only as a last resort when she was bored. She just wasn't bored a lot—who wanted to sit around all day when there were things to do?

Now Sarah's mom leaned down and kissed her on the forehead. Sarah could feel the glitter poking her skin. "Of course!" her mom said. "That's what I'm here for. I need to get back to work. Readers need things to read!" A flicker of doubt passed over her face. "Hmm. It occurs to me, in looking at this book I brought you, that this isn't the frontier." She sighed. "This might not be exactly what you were looking for. . . ."

Sarah got up and hugged her mom. "It's great, Mom."

Her mom squeezed her back. "My entrepreneur!" She let go of Sarah and said to herself, "Maybe a book on entrepreneurs? What about *Lean In* . . ." She walked out of the room, leaving eddies of glitter trailing after her. Sarah saw two handprints on the back of her mom's sweater where she'd hugged her.

Oh, well. Glitter made everything better.

Lizzie said, "I love your mom."

Sarah smiled. She knew what the rest of the sentence was: "I love your mom, but that didn't help us at all. Still, she's a really great mom and you're lucky." She thought there might have been a "And your flyers are the best" at the end of Lizzie's thoughts too.

Sarah looked at the clock. The grand opening of the stand was in a week, on the following Saturday. They needed to get the flyers out today, since Saturday was when most people in New Amity visited the stores on Main Street. "Let's get going. We need to get these up so everyone can see them!"

She could practically smell the ice cream. Candy swirl, bubble gum, chocolate peanut butter . . . When she looked at Lizzie, she knew she was feeling the same thing.

Lizzie grabbed the flyers and the tape. "Let's do some frontier marketing!"

Sarah burst out laughing.

"Where to first?" Lizzie asked, sweat already starting at her temples. Sarah knew she hated the summer. Not Sarah, though. The hotter the better. Still, she needed to get Lizzie to some air conditioning STAT.

"Okay, I have a plan," Sarah said, making up a plan as she spoke. "Um, we just zigzag down Main Street. It's better than hitting one side first." She sniffed so she sounded like she knew what she was talking about. She'd seen it in a movie once, maybe.

It didn't work. "Why?" Lizzie asked.

Sarah smiled. "I don't know. But it sounded good, right?"

Lizzie giggled and then puffed up her chest. She put on a British accent, immediately making herself sound hoity-toity. "Because everyone knows, dearest Sarah, that zigzagging is the only *civilized* way to put up flyers. Tally ho!"

They burst out laughing. Lizzie could do any voice at the drop of a hat. But she only ever did voices around Sarah. Which was fine with Sarah. She knew how awesome Lizzie was—who cared what anyone else thought? That was what being a best friend was about.

Sarah tried to mimic a British voice too, but it

just came out sounding like an alien new to Earth and to any kind of language. They doubled over laughing.

This was what the ice cream stand would be like every day. Best. Summer. Ever.

"Okay," Lizzie finally said. "Let's ask Sheriff Hadley first, since he's right across the street."

Sarah wrinkled her nose. She liked Sheriff Hadley, but he kept asking her mother out on dates. It was gross. Her mom and Sheriff Hadley on a date was almost as bad as Lizzie's parents holding hands.

Lizzie winked at her and then put her clasped hands under her chin. "Oh, Sheriff Hadley," she said, batting her eyelashes. "I'd love to go to a science fiction convention with you!"

Sarah snorted. Sheriff Hadley loved to dress

up for sci-fi conventions. He had more costumes than Sarah had ever worn for Halloween.

They walked across the street to the sheriff's building. The building had once been a one-room schoolhouse, but the sheriff's mom—former sheriff of New Amity—had converted it to a sheriff's station years ago. At least that was what he liked to tell Sarah's mom all the time. Sarah had no idea why.

When they opened the door, Sheriff Hadley was sitting at the desk, staring at the computer, occasionally running a hand through his bright red hair. Sarah could see a green tentacle waving on the screen. He was clearly watching a movie. A scream came through the speakers.

"SHERIFF HADLEY!" Sarah yelled, knowing it would startle him. He jumped so high, Sarah thought he might jump right out of his chair. Lizzie covered her mouth to keep from laughing, and this made Sarah laugh and then elbow her.

"Oh, hey, girls," Sheriff Hadley said. "How's Ana—I mean, your mom—Sarah?"

Sarah rolled her eyes.

"Fine. Anyway, we have flyers here for the ice cream stand. Can we post one on the bulletin board over there?" Sarah pointed to a board with a lot of WANTED posters on it that hung above a big cooler with a handmade sign that said BAIT—WORMS FOR SALE.

Sheriff Hadley looked at them thoughtfully. "Well, that might not be the best place for it. But we can tape it up right on the door to the outside."

Sarah and Lizzie smiled at each other. "That works!" Sarah said.

"Aren't you two a little young to be running the stand? I might have to arrest you for breaking the law. . . ." His eyes twinkled.

Lizzie's eyes got wide, but Sarah put her hands on her hips. "Good luck! I'm a fast runner." She pretend-glared at him. He pretend-glared at her. Then Sarah couldn't help it; she smiled. She felt Lizzie next to her breathe a sigh of relief.

"Oh, he's just kidding, Lizzie. Can we borrow your tape?" Sarah asked him.

"Fine," he said, sighing like it was a big hardship, then winking at Lizzie and Sarah. "So how come you get to run the stand this year, really? Aren't Gloria and Jeff doing it again?" He brought the tape over to them.

Lizzie said, "Camp," so softly a fly wouldn't be able to hear her, so Sarah jumped in. "Gloria is going to acting camp for a whole month of the summer. So WE get to take over."

Then Lizzie seemed to find her voice. She liked Sheriff Hadley—she just always needed Sarah to do the talking first. She said, "Oh, and because Gloria and Jeff aren't best friends anymore."

Sarah stopped and stared at Lizzie. Her mouth dropped open. She could feel her heart start galloping like a runaway horse, and she was pretty sure she heard a buzz in her ears. Gloria and Jeff, not best friends? That could even happen?? How could they STOP being best friends, just like that?

"But what happened?" she asked, her voice higher than she meant it to be.

Lizzie shrugged. "Gloria said they just grew apart. Something about . . . nothing in common? Or maybe she said he was a commoner? I can never tell with her. Anyway, she has a whole new group of acting friends now."

Sheriff Hadley smiled and said, "Well, that's too bad. Gloria marches to the beat of her own drummer, so let's hope she finds a great band that can match her style. But at least that means you two get to run the stand!"

Sarah could barely hear him. Why he was talking about drums at a time like this was beyond her, anyway. And why wasn't Lizzie as upset about this as she was? And why hadn't she told Sarah until now? If best friends could just STOP being best friends one day, that meant it could happen to Sarah and Lizzie.

Especially since they didn't have that much in common anymore.

Sarah tried to shake off her dread. They had

the ice cream stand for the whole summer. Then they had a zombie hayride. There was nothing and no one that would get in between them. That was that. They were best friends, always.

Still, the day felt different now. Suddenly, the air seemed frigid in the sheriff's office and the building felt really small.

Sarah cleared her throat and made herself stop thinking. To Sheriff Hadley she said, "And guess what?"

Sheriff Hadley put tape on the flyer and opened the door to the outside. Lizzie and Sarah followed him out.

"Uh, you are also going to start your own *Fortune* 500 company?" he said, centering the flyer on the door.

Sarah had no idea what that meant. "Of

course not. We'd never do that. But we ARE going to have a zombie hayride this fall, if we make enough money at the stand."

The sheriff gave the tape one last smooth and then turned to them. "A zombie hayride! Now that would be something."

"I KNOW!" Sarah practically shouted. "Lizzie and I went on one a couple of years ago and it was so. Much. Fun. We knew then we wanted to do one at the orchard. But we never could. Except this year, of course. Because we'll TOTALLY make enough money." Sarah didn't mention anything about her worries. The zombie hayride would be great. They had to make enough money. They had to. Suddenly she felt like a million ants were in her pants and she needed to move move move.

"Anyway! We gotta go. See ya!" She grabbed

Lizzie's hand and practically dragged her across the street.

"Thanks!" Lizzie called behind her, but Sarah kept dragging. Lizzie said, "Why are you going so fast?"

Sarah said, "We just need to get going." She didn't tell Lizzie she was really running away from the idea of losing her best friend.

CHAPTER 3

A Whole Bunch of Nuts Mixed
Together in a Small Bowl with Rainbow
Ice Cream. And Bait.

S arah, you're acting weird," Lizzie said.

"Not as weird as a zombie," Sarah said, then put her arms out and walked a zombie walk, groaning.

Lizzie laughed again. "Let's zombie-walk to Dinah's Diner."

They both stuck out their arms and shuffled along the street toward the diner. Two younger girls hanging around the farm supply store stared and pointed. Sarah recognized them from Community Spirit at the town hall on Sundays—Talia and Kateri. She whispered under her breath to Lizzie, "Let's give them a scare." Lizzie giggled but then groaned louder.

"Muuhhhhhhh! BRAINS!"

Sarah made her voice rough and loud and yelled, "I NEED LITTLE-KID BRAINS!" and then picked up the pace on her shuffling. Lizzie followed suit. Talia and Kateri squealed and laughed, then went sprinting away from them, giggling the whole time.

Something about the two of them made Sarah feel nostalgic. Maybe because they reminded her of Lizzie and herself when they were seven. Almost four long years ago. When things were simpler.

Sarah heard a jingle across the way and saw Hakeem walk out of Dinah's Diner (and Bait). She knew that meant he'd just dropped off some pastries. More importantly, she knew that Rachel might just give her and Lizzie a pastry so they could "test" it.

Sarah grabbed Lizzie's hand and pointed to Hakeem. Lizzie said, "Ohhh." Sarah and Lizzie stopped being zombies and took off toward the diner. Even though Lizzie hated running, everyone rushed for one of Hakeem's pastries.

They burst through the diner's doors. There were only a few people there—some from the town, but many from the surrounding towns. Sarah knew this because she knew everyone in New Amity.

"Hi, Rachel!" Sarah loved Rachel and Aaron, the part owners of Dinah's Diner (and Bait). They were pretty young for old people. She also loved Dinah, the actual owner and Aaron's grandma, who Sarah was pretty sure was older than all the adults in New Amity put together.

Rachel was hugely pregnant and always had one hand on her back. She stood up from putting the tray of pastries in the display at the front counter. "Just in time!" she said, smiling. "I think we have two pastries that need to be tested. Can you help?"

Sarah and Lizzie nodded solemnly. Sarah said, "Only if you post this flyer, though." Lizzie nudged Sarah with her elbow but also giggled. Sarah giggled a little too, but tried to keep a straight face. Fair was fair—they would *only* help Rachel by eating the pastries if she could help them. Still, she added, "Please."

"Sure! What is it?" Rachel walked around the

counter, carrying the two pastries on a little tray. Sarah and Lizzie grabbed the pastries and Sarah dug in without missing a beat.

Lizzie didn't mind doing the talking with Rachel because she was so nice, so she piped up, "It's a flyer for the ice cream stand. Sarah and I are going to run it this summer."

Aaron came out from the back, a white apron tied around him, streaked with all types of food. It said, KISS ME, I'M JEWISH. He smiled his nice smile at the girls. Sarah thought he was pretty okay-looking looking for an old person. He took a flyer. "Oh, aren't Gloria and Jeff doing it this year?"

Sarah practically choked on the pastry. She wanted to say: "No, Gloria abandoned her best friend." But she changed the subject, talking fast around a huge bite of pastry.

41

"Zshoombie ehright" was what it sounded like.

Lizzie translated, "She said 'zombie hayride.'"

Sarah swallowed. "We get to put on a zombie hayride if we make enough money."

Rachel's face clouded over. "I have to say, I'm not a fan of zombies," she said, rubbing her belly. "Just because this little one is a tad sensitive." Her face got green. "Uh-oh. I guess you can't even say it—" and with that, she hurried around the counter, her hand over her mouth.

Lizzie turned to Sarah. "We made her sick!"

Sarah took another bite of her pastry. "Whoops," she said, enjoying the raspberry filling.

Aaron watched helplessly as Rachel scurried away. "Poor Rachel," he said. "It's been like this her whole pregnancy. But only two more months." Dinah came over, walking slowly but with bright eyes. Sarah loved how twinkly they were.

"Well, two of my favorite girls are here and I still haven't gotten a hug?" she said, pulling Sarah in for a squeeze. Lizzie threw her arms around the two of them, making Sarah laugh. Dinah let them go with a pat and asked, "What brings you girls to the diner? It's summer vacation for you, right?"

Lizzie pointed to the flyer in Aaron's hand. "We were just asking Rachel and Aaron to post this."

Dinah took the flyer. "Oh, good! The ice cream stand. Hakeem's pastries are even better with ice cream, if you can believe it. But, say, aren't Gloria and Jeff doing it this year?"

Sarah pressed her lips together and suppressed a yell. Instead, she grabbed Lizzie's hand and pulled her out the door. Lizzie said, "Thanks!" as the door shut on the diner.

"What the—?" Lizzie started, but Sarah interrupted her.

"Hey, let's go to Hakeem's and post a flyer there."

Lizzie gave her a look, but Sarah pretended she didn't see. She practically ran to Hakeem's Sports Store and Hardware Plus Bait Shop next door to the diner, not even waiting for Lizzie. She breezed through the door, making the chime swing wildly. Sarah ran up to Hakeem, who was talking to Stella from Stella's Imported Goods and Local Bait Shop near the cash register.

"Hey! Hakeem! Will you post this?" Sarah said, out of breath yet still managing to yell.

"Excuse us, young lady," Stella said, looking down her nose and over her glasses at Sarah. Sarah thought Stella looked like she sucked on lemons every morning.

But still, she didn't mind that Stella interrupted her. Sarah was nice that way. "Oh, that's okay, Stella." To show she forgave her completely, Sarah held out a flyer to her. "Maybe you can post this flyer too."

The door chime went off again and Lizzie came up beside her. Sarah didn't look at her. Stella huffed but took the flyer, and Hakeem took one as well.

"You can't beat ice cream!" Hakeem said, and winked at Sarah.

Sarah said, "Yeah, Dinah says your pastries are even better with ice cream."

Stella spoke up. "How dare she! Hakeem's pastries are perfect as they are." She smiled adoringly at Hakeem. Sarah had to stop herself from rolling her eyes. Stella had been in love with Hakeem probably since before Sarah was even born, but Hakeem never seemed to notice. He was too preoccupied with his wife, who had passed away decades ago, to see anyone else around him.

Hakeem smiled kindly at Stella. "Oh, everything can be improved, that much we know. Dinah is a wise woman. In fact, maybe I'll concoct a pastry that goes perfectly with Garrison Family Orchard vanilla ice cream. My Camila loved ice cream!" He pointed to the photo of his wife he had put up on a wall of his store, right above a little altar. Sarah had seen it a million times—he pointed at it every time she came in. He put different decorations around it at different times, and there was always a string of lights around the photo. She gave Camila a little wave.

Stella sniffed. "It would be hard to improve upon your pastries, Hakeem, but I suppose it's always a worthy endeavor to improve ourselves. As I was saying before being interrupted"—Stella shot Sarah and Lizzie a dirty look—"I will bring you foods to freeze tonight, as I know you've been busy getting ready for Ramadan."

The door chime dinged again and Sarah saw Dani Alvarez enter. Dani was the town administrator.

But Sarah needed to get going. Her body needed to move move move—the more she stood around, the antsier she got. She REALLY didn't want to hear about Gloria and Jeff running the stand anymore. She started toward the door without looking at Lizzie and thrust a flyer at Dani. "Can you put this up in the town hall?" she asked, not even bothering to say hello.

"Oh, the stand! I just saw Gloria outside," said Dani.

Sarah closed her eyes, then opened them again. "Ughhh. She's not doing the stand this year. We are." She realized she'd said every word through clenched teeth.

Dani looked at her thoughtfully. "That's great, Sarah. It looks like maybe you've said this before."

Sarah huffed. "Like a million times! But we get to do it this year, and just because Gloria can't seem to keep—" She stopped herself to start over. "If we get enough money, we get to do a zombie hayride!"

Stella sniffed. "Well, I never."

Dani's eyes widened. "Ooh, I LOVE horror movies. What about a haunted house instead?"

Hakeem said, "Camila was never a fan of the scarier things. . . ."

Suddenly, Sarah felt close to tears. "Never mind," she grumbled, and walked fast to the door. This had started as such a good day. She loved the people in her town, and she'd thought everyone would be excited for them. Instead, everyone seemed to want to talk about Gloria or how much they hated the idea of a zombie hayride. Even Lizzie didn't seem to care as much today as Sarah wanted her to. Lizzie didn't seem bothered by anything.

Sarah did a quick wave behind herself at the adults and walked out the door. Lizzie followed close behind. Sarah could practically hear the question mark above her head.

They walked toward Annabelle's Antiques and Bait way down the road. A kid on a skateboard she didn't recognize zoomed close. Sarah almost knocked him over, she was walking so fast. "Hey, watch it!" he said, jumping off his skateboard. Sarah patted his back, at the same time taping a flyer to his T-shirt. The kid didn't notice and jumped on his skateboard and zoomed away. Lizzie giggled. Any other time, Sarah would have giggled too.

Up ahead of her, she saw a group of kids hanging around the antiques store but couldn't make out who it was quite yet.

"Sarah, are you going to tell me what's wrong?" Lizzie asked, puffing a little to keep pace.

Sarah shrugged. "I don't know. It's just . . . it seems like everyone was just . . ." She didn't quite know what she wanted to say. She looked down and slowed her walk a little. She could now hear the murmur of voices from the kids by the shop.

She really didn't want to get into a huge conversation with other people around. Especially when she wasn't sure what she wanted to say.

She wondered why kids were hanging around a boring old antiques shop, anyway. Ms. Henderson—Annabelle—liked to dress up in Regency dresses, long dresses that had puffed sleeves and a close-fitting top part. The rest of the dress was loose, like a really baggy, long tube. Sarah thought they actually looked comfortable, except for the top part. Ms. Henderson acted like a person in the early 1800s in a ton of other ways too. She often needed "smelling salts" because she had the "vapors," whatever all of that meant, and talked about "courting" and "consumption" a lot. In other words, Ms. Henderson was one of the stranger adults Sarah knew. Sarah thought all adults were a little weird, but Ms. Henderson was extra-special weird.

Lizzie gently touched her arm and Sarah stopped. "Do you feel like everyone was saying they'd miss Gloria at the stand? That sort of hurt my feelings too, if I'm honest."

Sarah started. That wasn't it at all! Of course they wouldn't MISS Gloria. No one would.

But before she could respond, she heard the word "ACTING!" yelled loudly. She turned to look. Now she could see the kids clearly—it was Gloria and her new group of acting friends. They were coming toward Lizzie and Sarah.

"Well, hello, baby children," Gloria said. She flipped a boa around her neck and looked down at them over her sunglasses. Three other kids stepped behind her. Sarah recognized Justin, Nyo, and Aisling from around town. They all wore little bits of costume: Justin had on steampunk glasses; Nyo wore a cape; and Aisling had on a crown.

Gloria went on, "You all know my baby sister, darlings. Lizzie, love, what brings you to this part of town?"

Sarah said, "Well, it's basically the only part of town? We're putting up flyers for the ice cream stand. You know, the one you used to run with your former best friend, Jeff?" She could feel Lizzie's eyes on her, but she kept her eyes forward.

Gloria nodded sagely. "Yes, ages ago my former best friend and I used to run the stand. Sometimes, one just transcends one's friends and must move on. No one knows when a person might outgrow another." She motioned to her group of friends, "But I have found my niche here. ACT-ING!" she yelled, and her three friends yelled,

53

"ACTING!" back. Then they all floated away, leaving Lizzie with a bewildered look on her face and Sarah completely unsettled.

When they were out of earshot, Lizzie said, "I love my sister, but she is so weird." She gave Sarah a look and said in exactly the same voice as Gloria, "ACTING!"

Sarah's anger began to ease up a little. Lizzie yelled the word again, then looked down her nose at Sarah and pranced around in a circle. Sarah started laughing and then doubled over as Lizzie pretended to throw a boa around her shoulder. "Well, helloooooo, baby children," she said in Gloria's voice. "You are such babies with your babyness. I can't possibly stand around with all the babies today."

Sarah started to snort. Lizzie joined her, and

pretty soon they were both out of breath and gasping for air from laughing. Sarah felt better—they were not Gloria and Jeff. They would never "outgrow" each other. Lizzie and Sarah were best friends forever.

Lizzie wiped her eyes and then got a serious look on her face. "I shouldn't be so mean," she said as she and Sarah started walking back through the town. "I'm really glad Gloria finally found the people she should be with. Friendships can't always last forever."

And with that, Sarah's good feeling melted away faster than an ice cream cone in the hot summer sun.

CHAPTER 4

Cotton Candy Ice Cream That Has Been
Best Friends with Birthday Cake Ice Cream
Forever Topped with Cherry-Flavored
Medicine and Sardines. Or, Things That
Shouldn't Get Lumped Together Ever.

The ice cream stand was going to open on Saturday, and by Thursday, Sarah felt like she was going to explode with all the waiting. Luckily, Lizzie had invited her and her mom over for dinner, which would kill some of the time. Not all, but some. Lizzie had hinted about a fun "surprise" that she knew Sarah would "die over." Sarah hoped it was something zombie-related.

Her mom couldn't go because of a dumb book

57

thing—Sarah didn't even know what it was—but she dropped Sarah off at 5:45 and told her she'd be back at 8:30.

"Be nice, Sarah," her mom said as Sarah opened the door of the car to get out.

Sarah gave her mom a puzzled look. "Why wouldn't I be nice?" she said.

Ms. Shirvani was digging through her purse. "Where did I put that . . ."

"Mom. MOM."

Finally, her mom looked up. "What, honey? Oh, here it is!" She pulled out some lipstick.

"Why wouldn't I be nice?" Sarah shut the door and leaned down to look through the window. "It's just Lizzie."

Sarah's mom put the car into reverse. "Oh, I just know that sometimes you can be a little . . .

possessive. I know you, that's all. Remember what it's like to be a newcomer. Gotta go, sweetie. Love you and see you soon!" She started backing up, and Sarah stood up straight, more confused than ever. But her mom was a little bit of a space cadet, so she wasn't too surprised. Her mom was a lot like Mr. Garrison, come to think of it.

Sarah heard a happy squeak and turned around. Lizzie was standing on the porch and waving at her excitedly. Sarah grinned and bounded to the porch, took the stairs in two huge strides (skipping two of them), and reached Lizzie.

"Well?" Sarah asked. This was a tradition before she ate dinner over at Lizzie's. Mr. G might be a little daydreamy, but he was one of the best cooks Sarah had ever met. She always wanted to hear about his concoctions before she actually went in to eat them. She swore it made them taste better.

"Um, apple butter bruschetta, apple walnut salad, curried carrot and apple soup, apple rosemary pork chops, and ice cream." Lizzie beamed at Sarah.

Sarah wrinkled up her nose. "But it's not even apple season yet. Why—"

Before she could get the question out, she heard Ms. G yell, "Girls, come set the table!" Sarah and Lizzie grinned and ran inside. They each hit the banister on the stairs three times and then rounded the corner to the kitchen.

The smells made Sarah want to do a happy dance. She was a little confused as to why there were so many apple dishes, since it wasn't fall, but they were at an orchard, after all. So she yelled,

"HEY, MR. G!" and got a mumble back, then grabbed some plates with Lizzie to put them out.

"Are you going to tell me the surprise?" Sarah asked. She'd almost forgotten to ask, what with the delicious smells, but she loved surprises. She put down some plates and then noticed that there were way too many. "Lizzie, there are nine plates here."

Lizzie was folding a napkin and adding the silverware. She looked up with a twinkle in her eyes. "I know!" Then she broke out in a huge smile.

"But there are only five of us," Sarah said. And then the doorbell rang.

"I'll get it, darlings!" she heard Gloria yell. Sarah thought it was probably some of her new acting friends.

Lizzie looked up. "Oh, they're here! Sarah, I just KNOW you're going to love them!" she squeaked.

"Huh?" Sarah said.

Voices rang in the hall. She heard everybody move to the dining room just as she and Lizzie put the finishing touches on the table.

In walked two grown-up men and two kids who looked to be about Sarah and Lizzie's age. The girl had on glasses and a spotless, prim sweater, perfectly matched with a skirt; she had huge brown eyes, medium-dark-brown skin, and curly hair in a bun on top of her head. The boy wore shorts and a *Dr. Who* T-shirt. He had the same skin tone and the same huge eyes, but his eyes were darting around everywhere. The girl pushed up her glasses and somehow looked down at everyone at the same time.

"Hey, Olive! Hey, Peter!" she heard Lizzie chirp. Sarah stared at her. She knew these kids?

Lizzie went and grabbed the girl's hand—Olive, evidently—and brought her in front of Sarah.

"Olive, this is my friend Sarah. Hey, Peter, come meet Sarah!" To Sarah, Lizzie said, "We met a while back when they came to visit New Amity and our orchard. They're twins. They are SO GREAT! We had a BLAST hanging out together. They love old movies just like me!"

Sarah felt a cold trickle of sweat travel down her back. Lizzie hadn't told her about them. Lizzie never hid anything from Sarah. And they'd already hung out and watched movies together, WITHOUT Sarah . . . She glanced at Gloria sitting on the stairs, looking at her fingernails and paying no attention to anyone. Was this how it had started with her and Jeff?

Lizzie went on, her voice high with excitement. "They're here from Boston with their dads for a whole year. John works at the university in Boston and studies apples. He's doing some kind of study with my mom and dad and the orchard. And his husband, Peter and Olive's other dad . . . does something else. What does he do, Olive?"

"He's an artist. How do you do?" Olive said to Sarah.

Sarah almost snorted. Olive sounded like she was a princess or something. A princess who looked down on everyone, clearly. Peter just kept looking around. Lizzie threaded her arm through Olive's, and Olive smiled at her.

Sarah did not like these two new people. She did not like them at all. They'd be here a whole YEAR?

She stuck her hand out. "Best friend," she said.

"What?" Olive said.

"I'm Lizzie's best friend." Sarah took Olive's hand and pumped it hard. When she released it, Olive massaged her hand.

Ms. G breezed in with David and John. "Sarah! I see you've met Olive and Peter! How wonderful! These very nice men are their dads, David and John Wu." Sarah shook their hands but avoided their eyes. Did they have to be here for a whole year?

"Hi, Mr. Wu and Mr. Wu," Sarah said.

"Oh, call me David." David had twinkly eyes and a kind face. It was hard not to immediately like him.

"And me, John." John looked like Olive. He even looked down his nose the way Olive just had.

65

"We've heard a lot about you, Sarah."

Olive spoke from near Sarah. "Tabitha, may I use your restroom?"

Sarah did a double take. Olive called Ms. G Tabitha? SARAH didn't even call her Tabitha. She didn't know why, exactly. Just that she'd called her Ms. G. for as long as she could remember.

"Certainly, honey. It's down that hall and to the left. You have to jiggle the handle a little." Ms. G smiled at Olive, and Olive walked—snottily, Sarah thought—away.

Mr. G came in, bearing a steaming tray of bruschetta. The smell wafted past Sarah, and her stomach growled.

"In honor of your study, John, I have prepared an apple-stravaganza!" he said, grinning. "Welcome to Garrison Family Orchard, the oldest orchard in New England! Everybody, grab a seat! This is just the beginning."

Sarah sincerely hoped not.

By the soup course, Sarah had had enough.

Gloria, wearing sunglasses and a boa, only talked about her new friends. Sarah tried to send her dirty looks, but she couldn't tell if they were received.

Worse, though: Olive and Peter and Lizzie seemed like they'd known each other for ages.

And no one had even asked her one question. She trailed her spoon in the soup and made the decision to NOT TALK to anyone. That would show them.

"So, Sarah, your mom is the librarian?" David looked at her with his nice eyes and smiled. Sarah shifted in her seat. Well, maybe she could answer just one question. . . .

"Yep! She wishes I'd read more, but it's summer and there are too many other things to do besides sit around all day." Sarah took a spoonful of the delicious soup and then remembered she was showing them all how mad they made her. But the taste was so good, she took another spoonful anyway.

David raised his eyebrows. "I know what you mean." He pointed his spoon at John. "This one keeps his nose in a book all day. I like to do things with my hands. So I make sculptures. I'm betting there will be an apple sculpture at the end of this year. You know, I always need an apprentice—you should stop by this summer if you're interested in helping!"

Sarah shook her head. "I can't. Lizzie and me are running the ice cream stand!" She smiled. "And if we get enough money, we'll get to do a zombie hayride in the fall!" Sarah got so excited, she knocked her spoon out of the soup and splattered some on her place mat.

"A zombie hayride?" Peter stared at Sarah. "That would be so cool!" Sarah couldn't believe he actually talked.

Lizzie made her squeak noise, which meant "*I KNOW.*" So Sarah said it out loud for her. "I KNOW," but she directed it at Lizzie.

"Oh, these two would love something like that. Especially if it was based on a classic movie." John elbowed Peter for emphasis.

Olive, holding her spoon snottily (again according to Sarah), said, "Oh, yes, we'd like that

69

very much! We tend to like campy horror films. That's what Peter means."

Sarah scoffed. She didn't think Olive had to speak for Peter. That seemed weird.

Lizzie scrunched her eyebrows at Sarah. "Sarah doesn't like old movies. Gloria got me into them a while back. I had so much fun watching them with Olive and Peter!" Sarah glared at everyone at the table.

Gloria said, "Yes, one must teach one's sister good taste," and then swung the boa over her shoulder. Even though she had to take it off her shoulder, bring it down, and then throw it over her shoulder again to do it.

Sarah swallowed. "It's not that I don't like them . . . ," she muttered.

Lizzie laughed. "That's not true! Remember

the last time we tried to watch them? You just kept saying how weird they talked. And then fell asleep."

The whole table laughed, and Sarah's face burned. She stared at Lizzie—what was happening?

Peter spoke up. "Olive can do those old-movie voices. I can too, but not as great as Olive."

Everyone—everyone but Sarah—looked at Olive expectantly. She smiled and put her spoon down. "Peter, let's do the thing!" Peter nodded and laughed.

David's crinkly eyes crinkled up even more, and even John sat back. This was clearly something Olive and Peter did for their family a lot.

Olive cleared her throat. Then she said, in one of the best old-movie voices Sarah had ever heard, "I say, what's the meaning of this, see? There's no such thing as zombies. If you keep spouting that hooey, we'll put you in the booby hatch faster than you can say 'rube'!"

Peter said, in another amazing old-movie voice, "What's the big idea? Youse a wiseacre or something? Shut your pie hole and beat it before I start yapping to the coppers!"

The entire table cracked up.

Lizzie laughed and caught Sarah's eye. Then she took a deep breath and said in another old-movie voice, "This is a hootenanny, if I've ever seen one. Say, these kids ain't half bad!" And the table roared with laughter again.

Except for Sarah. Lizzie never did her voices for anyone else. Ever. Only for Sarah. But now it seemed like Sarah didn't know Lizzie at all; she hadn't told her about Gloria and Jeff, she hadn't told her about Olive and Peter, and she suddenly didn't seem to have a problem pointing out to the whole table how dumb Sarah was. Sarah could feel her entire friendship turning upside down. This was the worst thing ever.

Or almost the worst.

Lizzie went on, this time in her real voice, "Oh my gosh, Peter and Olive! I have the BEST idea. If you two don't know what to do this summer, you should come help us at the ice cream stand! We could talk about movies and the zombie hayride all summer!"

CHAPTER 5

*Too Many Weird Flavors All
Bumping into Each Other and Ruining
EVERYTHING. Plus Sprinkles.*

The day of the stand opening, Sarah had a hard time getting going.

"Honey," her mom said, shaking her again. "You're going to be late. You don't want to be late on the first day, do you?"

"Mmfffsshsshherrbbbeerrrtttt," Sarah said into her pillow.

Her mom said, "That is a good point. But you

can't hide from the day forever. The day happens anyway, you know."

Sarah flopped over and blew a clump of her dark brown hair out of her eyes. "It's just . . ."

Her mom had been in the middle of getting up, but she sat back down. Sarah played with the coverlet her grandma had made for her.

"It's just . . . ?" her mom said softly.

"Peter and Olive are going to ruin everything. This was supposed to be for me and Lizzie. And Lizzie went ahead and asked them to join us without asking me."

Her mom took a sip of coffee and looked away. "You know, your grandma and grandpa were new once. To this whole country. They came all the way from Iran. And some other people didn't want them here either."

Sarah started to roll her eyes—she'd heard this before. But she immediately felt bad. She knew Nane and Papa had had a hard time. She looked down at the comforter.

Her mom went on, "But there were kind people everywhere. And my mother decided she would concentrate on the good in the people around her. Do you think you can find out what the good things about Peter and Olive are? And concentrate on that? I know!" her mom said suddenly, even bouncing Sarah on the bed a little. Sarah eyed the coffee nervously. "You can make it seem like a mystery! Like you're finding clues."

Sarah shrugged, though it was hard since she was still lying down. She blew imaginary hair out of her eyes.

Her mom stopped bouncing and got a serious

look on her face. "And can you think about what it's like to be new?"

Sometimes her mom and Lizzie were so much alike, Sarah could hardly believe it. She bet that was exactly what Lizzie had been thinking when she'd invited Peter and Olive. It was just like Lizzie to think about how other people felt. Remembering them laughing so hard about old movies and talking about how Sarah didn't like them made her burn with anger.

But thinking of Nane and Papa, Sarah thought maybe her mom and Lizzie were right. She was so confused.

She felt awful, and mad, and sad, and scared. Her mom always told her to pay attention to her feelings. So which one was she supposed to pay attention to?

Her mom stood up. "All right, sleepyhead. Up and at 'em! It's time to scoop some ice cream!" She got a dreamy look in her eye. "Ooh! I know just the book for this mystery: Trixie Belden!" She disappeared out of the room, moving so fast that some coffee sloshed on the floor.

Sarah flipped her legs over the edge of the bed and put her feet in the fluffy rug, which now had drops of coffee on it. She could also see flecks of glitter here and there.

"Okay," she said to the room. "I'm going to MAKE this day be good. I'm going to see the good in"—she swallowed—"Peter and Olive. And in this whole situation." She picked up her stuffed unicorn—Sparkles—and said, "This day is going to be great. I'm sure Olive and Peter are"—she clenched her teeth—"fine. And ice cream is good. And I am going to have the best day—and summer—ever."

Even Sparkles didn't look like he believed that.

By the time Sarah started biking to the stand, she felt two overwhelming things: mad and sad. So she rode fast and slow, then fast and slow. Her heart beat fast, and it had nothing to do with the bike ride. She wondered what she would say to Lizzie. She'd never been mad at Lizzie before. She wasn't sure what to do.

When she got close to the stand, Sarah saw Lizzie's dad bustling around it. At first she thought he was talking to himself—he did that a lot—but then she heard Olive's voice coming from the back of the stand, in the freezer part.

Sarah started pedaling faster without realizing it. She rode up to the stand so fast and stopped so hard that her bike kicked up dirt—all over Lizzie's dad.

"Mr. G! I'm so sorry!" Sarah jumped off her bike and let it fall, but then she wasn't sure what to do.

He gave her a huge smile. "I love the enthusiasm!" He took off his glasses and wiped them down.

Lizzie, Peter, and Olive opened the door in the back and came out. Sarah narrowed her eyes. They'd all gotten there before her. Probably all becoming best friends. Lizzie waved at Sarah, but Sarah pretended not to see it.

As Mr. Garrison put his handkerchief back in his pocket, he said, more to himself than to anyone else around him, "What's this . . . ?"

He took a piece of paper out of his pocket and unfolded it. His face brightened. "Oh! I saw this

the other day when I was in Boston getting supplies. I meant to give it to you at dinner the other
day. Totally slipped my mind! Too many good
movie impressions, I think!" He winked at Olive
and Peter. Sarah could feel that Lizzie was still
looking at her, but she couldn't bring herself to
look back. "Thank goodness I didn't wash these
pants!" Mr. G said.

Sarah wrinkled her nose. Lizzie said,
"Dad . . . ," which meant "GROSS." Sarah whole-
heartedly agreed.

Mr. Garrison handed Sarah the piece of
paper, and she took it reluctantly. She'd just be
sure to wash her hands REALLY well before
scooping any ice cream. Lizzie came over and
stood next to her, reading the flyer. Sarah took a
tiny step over so they weren't quite so close.

ATTENTION, ICE CREAM LOVERS!

MOO is having its 5th Annual Sundae Contest for Boston and surrounding areas!

The Skinny: Submit your favorite ice cream sundae idea and win $5,000! The winner will also be the "Sundae of the Summer" and will have a permanent place on MOO's menu each and every year!

The Details: Sign up to show your stuff! Three judges will decide the winner in a tasting contest on June 22.

Sarah shrugged and passed the flyer over to Lizzie. This didn't really matter. They'd make enough money for the zombie hayride at the ice cream stand. Maybe she'd enter MOO's contest anyway. She could use a new bike. And maybe even a new best friend to ride it with. She swallowed a wave of sadness and said, "Thanks, Mr. G."

Sarah took a deep breath and tried to remember what her mom had said. She finally looked at Lizzie and then gave her and everyone else as big a smile as she could muster.

Olive, looking over her glasses, the round black frames already sliding down her nose, said, "We should start prepping. The stand opens in ten minutes."

Sarah's smile turned into a scowl. "I know that," she said. "Let's go."

"Good luck, kids!" Mr. G said. "We expect great things from the four of you, now!" He walked away, muttering to himself. Sarah didn't glance at him and strode toward the back of the stand. She could feel everyone following her as she opened the door and stepped inside.

The front of the stand was an open counter that held buckets of ice cream behind a plexiglass guard. The cash register was at one end—old and weird and still hard for Sarah to use. The roof extended over the counter and out about five feet, held up by long wooden posts. That gave the counter and some customers shade, but not enough so that people could hang around or sit down anywhere. Sarah was super-glad there weren't tables they'd have to clean up. The rest of the stand was behind a door, just behind the cash register—that door was the only way in and out of the front of the stand. The back was where the big freezers were, along with some long metal tables used for prep work. The hard part was how tiny it was. Sarah hadn't realized just how tiny until all four of them squeezed in together. In fact, there seemed to be two extra people in there.

Sarah took another deep breath and was about to speak when Olive said, "Okay, Lizzie and I will grab the ice cream flavors, and, Peter, you and Sarah grab the toppings."

Sarah huffed. But the directions made sense, so she shot Olive a dirty look and started grabbing the toppings. She could feel Lizzie still looking at her, but she couldn't meet her eyes.

No one talked. The generator hummed in the background. The ice cream stand was supposed to be way more fun than this. But in ten minutes, the stand was set up and all four of them were standing around in their aprons.

Finally, Sarah felt excited. She had been looking forward to this all spring. She caught Lizzie's eye and gave her a little smile. Lizzie's whole face brightened, and she gave Sarah a huge, relieved smile in return. They all heard the bell by the counter ding—their first customers!

Then Olive said, "Why don't Lizzie and I scoop the ice cream, Peter can do the toppings, and you can do the register?"

Sarah felt her face get hot. Of course Olive wanted to scoop ice cream with HER best friend. Instead of keeping quiet, though, she put her hands on her hips. "Why don't Lizzie and *I* scoop—" but then she stopped. Either Sarah or Lizzie had to work the register, since they were the only ones who knew how. Olive and Peter probably hadn't gotten trained yet. And Olive's plan made the most sense . . . again.

So Sarah said, "Duh," and quietly moved to the register. Lizzie gave her an anxious smile and a look that said, "Sorry, but this makes the most sense, and anyway, you're a math genius so you might as well be at the register." Sarah couldn't really argue with that.

They all walked out to the counter.

The first customer was a mother of what looked like twenty kids who kept running around, yelling. Sarah didn't recognize her but got a thrill from realizing that their flyers must have worked. The mother started her order. "Okay. We'll have two vanilla cones with chocolate dip and sprinkles; two chocolate sundaes with Reese's Pieces . . ."

Halfway through the order, Sarah felt a little panicked. When the mom finally stopped and stared at them expectantly, Peter, Olive, Sarah, and Lizzie all stood there, mouths wide open.

Then Olive and Sarah started barking orders at the same time.

Sarah said, "Lizzie, start with the sundaes, then end with the dip cones—"

At the same time that Olive said, "Lizzie, do the sundaes first so Peter can figure out the toppings—"

"Peter, write down the toppings list—"

"Peter can remember the toppings—"

And then the little kids waiting for the ice cream started screaming. Sarah wasn't sure what happened next. Everything moved so fast that she wasn't sure who was doing what, though she was relieved to see that Peter seemed to remember every single topping and what it went with—no one else could do that. Meanwhile, she tried to help scoop with Lizzie before she had to ring everything up, but she and Olive kept bumping into each other, at one point bonking heads so hard, Sarah saw stars.

Finally, after what seemed like ages, Sarah rang the whole order up and the family with the screaming kids went away. Sarah looked at Olive, Lizzie, and Peter. Every one of them had chocolate smeared on their faces. Lizzie had Reese's Pieces in her hair and Olive had something smudged on her glasses. Peter had cookie dough on his eyebrow. Sarah looked down and found a row of M&M's on her apron's waistband. She was already exhausted.

And then she remembered they'd only helped one customer. She looked up and saw the line snaking across the orchard. She saw the sheriff, and Stella, and Hakeem, and Rachel, and a ton of people she didn't even recognize. She looked at Lizzie and Lizzie looked back and both of them swallowed big. This would be a long day.

Olive jumped in between their looks. "Uh, we have more customers?" she said. Sarah closed her eyes and just nodded.

Chocolate
cone $1.00

CHAPTER 6

*Banana Split with Vanilla, Cherry, and
Chocolate Fudge Ice Cream, Drizzled with
Strawberry Sauce and a Whole Bunch
of NUTS. Plus Whipped Cream.
Plus Someone Selling Bait.*

The next few customers were people Sarah recognized. Stella ordered a small vanilla cone and said, "Well, I order this hoping I'm not contributing to some gauche zombie something or other." She took a taste and turned to Hakeem behind her. "Hakeem, this would only ruin your amazing baking." But she looked back at Peter and Olive. "Welcome, young people. The town of New Amity is thrilled to have you."

Sarah couldn't help thinking, "Not the whole town," but she didn't say anything out loud.

Next came Rachel and Aaron. Rachel ordered one of the biggest sundaes Sarah had ever seen. Aaron laughed, "That's bigger than your head!" and Rachel gave him such a dirty look that Sarah ducked her own head.

Rachel said, "I tell you what, honey, you can talk about my ice cream choices when YOU are growing our baby."

Aaron shrank back. He cleared his throat. "I think it's a PERFECT sundae. Just perfect. And anyway, we should spend our money now before the baby comes and we have no money left!" He winked at the crew behind the counter. "Olive and Peter, come by the diner. We'll give you a free pastry and drink—our town is so happy to have you here!"

Sarah rolled her eyes. They never gave HER a free pastry and drink. Well, barely. Maybe only every other time she came in. Or every time. The specifics weren't important.

Hakeem ordered a sundae and smiled big at Peter and Olive, saying, "Stop at the store anytime! I'll introduce you to Camila."

Mariko and Aldo, owners of the Farm Supply Store Plus Oil Change (and Bait) Shop, were next. They complained about the slow summer months at the store and even ordered a double-dip cone each. All of them offered Olive and Peter free things at their stores. This made Lizzie beam but made Sarah feel invisible.

Sheriff Hadley got to the head of the line. "Hey, Sarah!"

Sarah perked up a little. "Hey, Sheriff." Finally,

someone remembered who she was.

Then the sheriff turned to Olive and Peter. "Well, we are so excited to have you in town. If you want a tour of the town from someone who's lived here forever, I'd be happy to show you around!"

Sarah clenched her teeth. "I want to go on a tour!" she said.

But Sheriff Hadley laughed. "What are you talking about, Sarah? You know this town better than I do." He tipped his hat at Olive and Peter, winked at Lizzie, ignored Sarah, and walked away.

Finally, the line had ended. Olive said, "You know, they were all complaining about how slow things have been for them. But then they all bought ice cream."

Sarah turned on her. "So?" she said.

Olive shrugged. "I don't know. Either they

really like ice cream or they really like you guys."

Sarah didn't say, "Or they really wanted to say hi to you and pretend I don't exist."

But she wanted to.

"How much longer until we close?" Olive asked.

Lizzie glanced at the clock. "Fifteen minutes." Then her face brightened. "You know, there are no customers. And the bonus part of this job is getting to eat ice cream. . . ."

Suddenly, Sarah wasn't tired anymore. "So let's eat ice cream!" she practically yelled. Peter and Olive shared a smile.

Olive's eyes lit up. "I would like that very much."

Sarah had to stop from rolling her eyes at her. She just said things so weird.

The four kids each grabbed an ice cream scoop and picked out their ice cream. Lizzie got her double-dip cone with Butterfinger coating and Sarah had her bubble gum sundae with chocolate syrup and candy canes. Olive wrinkled her nose when she saw her make it. So Sarah made it extra big.

Olive, she saw, had a very neat cone with one scoop of mint chocolate chip ice cream. As far as Sarah was concerned, Olive might as well have been 100. Only old people got that flavor. She tried to share a look with Lizzie, but Lizzie was too busy trying to keep the Butterfinger chunks on her cone from falling off.

To Sarah's surprise, Peter had a gigantic sundae with about twelve different toppings on it. When Sarah looked at him, he grinned, a smile so big, it lit up his face. She couldn't help it—she grinned back. A little.

"Excuse me?" a voice called out, startling Sarah so much, she almost dropped her sundae. She looked up and saw the cutest boy around her age she'd ever seen. He looked familiar. His skin was a rich tawny brown, just a little darker than Sarah's. His hair was mussed but with some gel in it, and he had the longest eyelashes. Plus, he was wearing a really cool outfit—like maybe she'd seen on a TV show. He seemed way more polished than anyone from New Amity.

"Who are you?" she asked, more loudly than she meant to. Then she cleared her throat. "I mean, what can we help you with?"

She glanced at Lizzie. Lizzie had Butterfinger chunks all around her lips. Her eyes were wide and her cheeks were turning bright red. She was always a little pink to begin with, so when she blushed, the red took over her entire face. "Ice cream," she said.

Sarah, Olive, and Peter all looked at her. Lizzie stood up taller and said, "I mean, ice cream . . ." Her words trailed off.

Sarah was a little worried. Sometimes Lizzie didn't have the right words to say, but she never just said random words at people.

Olive piped up, "Can we get you some ice cream?" Lizzie gave Olive a relieved look, sparking another pang of irritation in Sarah.

The boy said, "I'm Beckett. It's nice to meet you. How long have you been running this ice cream stand?"

Sarah frowned. Was he trying to say they weren't very good at it? "Uh, none of your beeswax, that's how long," she said.

Lizzie stammered at the exact same time, "Th-three hours and f-forty-five minutes."

Olive jumped in. "We just started. I think this is the first summer for all of us."

She wasn't wrong, but still, Sarah couldn't let that go. "This is the first summer in New Amity for Peter and Olive. And at the *orchard,* too. Lizzie and I live here. Or, Lizzie lives here. I practically do. We've been friends since we were babies. It's like my orchard too." She cleared her throat when she realized everyone was looking at her.

The boy smiled and trained his gaze on Lizzie. "This is your family's orchard? Have you had it long?"

Lizzie nodded. The Butterfinger chunk fell off, and when it landed, Lizzie gasped and quickly wiped her face.

"They've had it since the 1800s, basically," said a voice Sarah barely recognized. It was Peter. Finally, he was talking, and not in old-movie voices that delighted Sarah's favorite people and left her out. Peter went on. "The Garrisons built this orchard in 1731 and have had someone in their family running it since then. They were one of the first orchards to really start diversifying their apple trees and were the first orchard in New England to start growing the Baldwin, the Davey, and the Ginger Gold." Peter smiled and gave a little nod. Sarah stared at Peter, dumbfounded. And he wasn't even done.

"Garrison Family Orchard also has a pumpkin patch and harvest festival in the fall, Christmas trees and a baked goods bazaar and contest in the winter, and sleigh rides all through the winter weekends. In the spring, there's a spring equinox celebration and a Mother's Day picnic, and there's almost always pick-your-own stuff going on. And, of course, in the summer, there's this ice cream stand." He took a gigantic bite of his sundae.

Sarah looked at Olive. She had a small smile on her face. Like she was proud. "Peter knows stuff. He remembers everything. He studied up on this orchard before we came."

Sarah hadn't known any of the history of the orchard. Except that it was old. And had apples.

Olive kept going. "And he's really good at math, and is awesome at robotics. He's good at everything." Peter elbowed her and gave her a look. "What?" she said. "You are."

"That's really cool," Beckett said. He looked again at Lizzie, who had smeared the Butterfinger on her chin. "Do you make a lot of money at this ice cream stand?"

Sarah jumped in before anyone else could. "Yeah. We're going to be able to do a whole zombie hayride in the fall if we make enough money."

Lizzie finally came to life. "Yes! So we have to work extra hard. Sarah and I have been asking for this for forever. Halloween is the best holiday, we think." Then she glanced at Beckett again and her cheeks got even redder.

Peter said, "Me too!" and Olive said "Me too!" at the exact same time.

Beckett nodded. "Okay, thanks so much, guys," he said. "I'll see you around." Then he turned and walked away, without any ice cream.

Sarah and Lizzie shared a look, Sarah temporarily forgetting she was still mad.

"Who was that guy?" Olive asked. "Was he an eighth grader?"

Lizzie shrugged but looked after him dreamily.

Sarah answered. "He must go to Hanoverville. He's probably in eighth grade at their middle school. Maybe Gloria knows him."

"Well, he seemed a little weird, asking all those questions," Olive said.

Sarah, who thought the exact same thing, said, "I didn't think so at all. Evidently you don't know anything about the people around here." Then she took off her apron and walked to the back, smiling to herself.

CHAPTER 7

One Cone. All Alone. And . . .
BETRAYAL. But Maybe a Couple of
Other Scoops Could Help?

For two weeks, things stayed pretty much the same. Sarah came to the ice cream stand to find Peter, Olive, and Lizzie all laughing. And she went home feeling like her best friend was miles away.

If she was still her best friend.

Even Sarah's mom noticed the way she moped around the apartment. Every once in a while she'd say, "You haven't spent the night at Lizzie's lately. . . ." But Sarah would always move away fast and pretend she had to do something else. Once, she even went and shelved books without being asked. Her mom checked her forehead for a fever.

Peter had taken over the cash register because he loved it and because he remembered the prices of everything without having to look them up. That should have given Sarah more time with Lizzie, scooping ice cream, but she ended up spending a lot of time in the back, near the freezers. What she was secretly doing was counting the money. If they could just get enough money . . . if they could just get a zombie hayride going, maybe Lizzie would remember that SARAH was her best friend, and not the new kids who everyone seemed to love more than Sarah.

On the Saturday two weeks into their time at

the stand, with only five minutes left before clos-
ing, Sarah went to the back to count the money
again before everyone started putting things away.
They had over $2,000 in the safe. Mr. G. came and
took what money was needed for supplies and left
any profit so they could keep track of how much
they'd earned so far. And they were almost halfway
there—and it was only the middle of June! That
meant that they would totally make the $5,000.
And she and Lizzie could plan for the hayride all
through July. The idea of getting her best friend
back made a zing go through her.

She entered in the safe's combination—the
year the orchard first started—and swung open
the door.

The safe was empty.

Sarah gasped. She put her hand in the safe

and felt all around. There was nothing in it. All the money was gone.

Sarah shrieked and yelled, "WHAT IN THE HOLY . . ."

Olive, Peter, and Lizzie came rushing in.

"Sarah, are you okay?" Lizzie asked.

Sarah shook her head. "No. No, I'm not okay. Look." She pointed to the safe. Lizzie bent down, looked in, then stood straight up, her face white as a sheet.

Olive asked, "What's going on?" She bent down and looked inside the safe. "Is there normally stuff in there?"

Sarah groaned. "Oh, only all our money. You know. Something small like that."

Olive's eyes got huge behind her glasses. Peter made an O with his mouth. Lizzie squeaked.

"All of it?" Olive asked.

Sarah didn't even answer. She slumped against the metal table. She and Lizzie looked at each other, fully, maybe for the first time in weeks.

Lizzie said, "That means . . ."

Sarah just nodded.

Olive asked impatiently, "That means what?"

Sarah didn't understand why SHE was impatient. So she answered back just as impatiently, "It means that we can't have a zombie hayride after all."

Olive pushed her glasses up her nose. "Oh. That's all. I thought you meant you knew the thief. Because we've been robbed and that's the big deal, you know."

Sarah stood up straight. "Duh! I was just jumping ahead to what it actually means for us."

Even Lizzie looked at Olive like she was from a different planet.

Olive looked at both of them. "It just doesn't seem like it's that—" But Peter elbowed her and gave her a look. She gave him a look back. Finally, she seemed to get it.

"Oh, this is something you've wanted for a long time so it's a big deal to you," Olive finally said.

Sarah rolled her eyes and shook her head, but she saw Lizzie give a sad smile to Olive. For the first time, Sarah wondered if Lizzie was sad that she and Sarah had grown so far apart. And then was sad that they wouldn't have the zombie hayride to bring them back together.

Or worse. They wouldn't be able to run the ice cream stand at all anymore. Even though it had been uncomfortable for her for two weeks, the thought of it being taken away made her shiver.

Lizzie said, "We have to . . . ," but she trailed off.

Sarah knew she was thinking they had to tell Lizzie's parents. But an idea was growing in her head. "I don't know, Lizzie. Maybe not."

Olive shook her head and half-smiled. "People say this to Peter and me and now I think I get it: 'You know, the rest of us can't read your minds!'" She looked genuinely amused. Sarah looked at Lizzie. Olive went on, "You guys do that, you know. Lizzie will start a sentence and not finish it, and then, Sarah, you'll answer her like she did. We don't know the rest of the sentence. We're over here, left out."

Sarah gaped at them. She clenched her fists. "YOU feel left out? YOU—" she started.

But Lizzie interrupted. "Sarah, what did you mean? What are you thinking?"

Sarah closed her eyes and breathed. She tried to imagine what it was like for Olive and Peter, the way her mom had told her to. She tried to hear what Olive had just said, that they thought Lizzie and Sarah had a special relationship. That part felt good. So maybe there was something to work with here. . . .

"Listen, you guys," Sarah said. "We need to tell Mr. and Ms. G about the money. But not yet. I say we do a little investigation of our own first. If we can't find the money in the next day or so, we tell your parents, Lizzie. But we have to give this a shot. What do you think? We can"—she swallowed a little—"work together to find the culprit."

It was quieter after Sarah's speech than she'd

hoped. She shifted on her feet. Lizzie chewed on her finger.

But Peter smiled. "Yep. I think that's a great idea."

Olive shrugged. Then a shy smile grew on her face. "We should definitely get the *scoop* on what happened!"

Sarah groaned, but she also laughed a little. That was a little funny, anyway. Not too bad for a new girl. Who saw everything wrong. And was a know-it-all.

Lizzie was still quiet.

"Lizzie?" Sarah was used to interpreting what Lizzie meant, but this type of quiet was a new thing. Finally, Lizzie stopped chewing her finger, her face more determined than Sarah had ever seen it.

"We are DEFINITELY a team," Lizzie said. She looked at Sarah when she said it. "Always. Let's do it." Then she smiled so big, it made every single one of them smile back.

After some conversation, they had all decided it was probably Beckett. He was the only one who had asked about how much money the stand made.

Everybody was convinced except Lizzie.

"It has to be him," Sarah said. "He probably snuck back there while we were getting our ice cream. Who else could it be?"

"Lots of people," Lizzie said, crossing her arms.

Sarah groaned and bit back about a thousand things she wanted to say. Things like "I think you just like him." And "I don't think you're being smart about this." And "I really want your T-shirt."

Olive pushed up her glasses. "Lizzie, remember, he *is* the only one who asked any sort of questions."

The four of them were sitting cross-legged on top of a picnic table that stood by the creek in the orchard. Sarah had grabbed a handful of long grass and was tying each stem into knots. Peter stared straight up at the trees—Sarah thought he was probably counting leaves. She'd done that a few times herself.

Lizzie shook her head. "I just think he was curious! He thought the orchard was interesting, that's all."

Sarah threw the piece of grass twisted in a knot and watched the breeze take it. Poor Lizzie. She was totally in love. Sarah tried to make her voice soft. "Do you really think most kids are interested in an orchard?"

Olive piped up, "Well. To be fair, we were."

Sarah looked at her and she shrugged. Olive added, "But I don't think most kids would be, Lizzie, sorry."

Lizzie jutted her chin out and Sarah thought, "Uh-oh." Because when Lizzie did that, it meant "I'm not going to listen" and "You can talk all you want, but I'm right" and "Sure, I'll lend you my T-shirt." The last part might have been Sarah making things up.

Sarah sighed. "Okay, let's say that boy from yesterday was just asking questions because he liked orchards. Then why would he care about how much money we make?"

Olive nodded. "Right. Lizzie, we don't have to accuse him or anything. I have a different idea."

Sarah's eyebrows shot up. She wondered if

Olive was going to boss him around until he confessed. Or move into Hanoverville and take over an ice cream stand there and make everyone like her better and steal his best friend.

"What was his name again?" Olive asked.

Peter elbowed Olive and pointed at the tree and they shared a private laugh. Clearly an inside joke. Sarah had to admit this was a little annoying and was a lot like her and Lizzie—or like they used to be. She'd always thought she and Lizzie could be twins. Even though Lizzie had pale skin and was a little short and marshmallowy, where Sarah had beige-brown skin and was beanpoley.

Lizzie said, "Um, his name is Beckett McIntyre." She blushed.

Peter said, "He told us his last name?"

Olive shook her head at him and for a minute, maybe Sarah actually liked Olive. She didn't want Lizzie to be embarrassed. Because the boy most definitely had not said his last name. Which probably meant Lizzie had asked Gloria about him after he'd left.

The blush on Lizzie's skin got deeper.

Sarah cleared her throat. "So what's your plan, Olive?"

Olive nodded excitedly and pushed up her glasses again. "Okay, how about this? He stole a bunch of money, right? So maybe he's spending it in town. We can ask the businesses if there have been any big spenders. Or, if we can find him, we can follow him. Maybe there's a perfectly good reason he asked questions. Or maybe he just bought himself something great."

"What if he spent the money already?" Peter asked.

Lizzie shook her head. "He didn't take it." Her chin was still out.

Sarah ignored her comment and said, "There probably hasn't been enough time to spend it."

Lizzie hopped off the table, startling Sarah so much, she dropped all the grass she was holding. It slipped away through the cracks in the picnic table.

Lizzie said, "Okay. We follow him. But after a little bit, I think we need to just ask him. Maybe he even has an idea of who could have taken the money."

Sarah rolled her eyes, but Lizzie caught her, so she tried to make it look like she was doing eye exercises.

"Are you okay?" Olive asked her. "Your eyes are looking weird."

Sarah just nodded and cleared her throat.

She jumped off the picnic table too. "Okay, deal. Tomorrow we'll go into town and try to pick up the trail of Beckett McIntyre. We can start the investigation then."

Olive patted Lizzie's shoulder. "He might still be good boyfriend material, Lizzie."

Lizzie's face got so red, Sarah thought she might explode. All Sarah's goodwill toward Olive disappeared. Sarah glared at her.

But Olive said, "What? Oh, for Pete's sake. Can we just say it? It's nothing to be embarrassed about. Lizzie likes Beckett McIntyre."

Lizzie flopped back down on the picnic table bench and covered her face with her hands. "Do not," Sarah heard her say.

Peter chuckled and sat down next to Lizzie.

He patted her shoulder. "Listen. He's DEFI-NITELY cute."

Lizzie dropped her hands and looked at Peter. Sarah knew that look meant "Are you kidding?" and "Are you making fun of me?" And, probably, "That shirt WOULD look good on Sarah, you're right."

Peter grinned at her. Lizzie grinned back. "Yeah, he is."

Sarah's jealous feelings flared and she couldn't help herself. "Yeah, yeah. He's cute. Is this a plan or what?"

Lizzie smiled at her, her embarrassment seemingly gone. "Yes. Let's go follow Beckett McIntyre."

CHAPTER 8

Peach Ice Cream Scoops with
Mango Bits and Chopped-Up Almonds.
Plus Some Sour Cherry Candy Bits
That You Never See Coming.

The next day, the four of them met up and biked into town together. After only half an hour of wandering around, looking for their suspect, they got a miraculous break.

Beckett McIntyre.

Lizzie had spotted him about a mile away, going into Annabelle's Antiques and Bait, carrying a huge package under his arm. Sarah could hardly believe it.

The four of them raced to the shop. They dropped their bikes behind the building, trying to be as quiet as they could. Sarah pointed to the back door—she knew it was always open. She'd helped Ms. Henderson carry things through it during the day more than once. She made motions with her hands that were supposed to look like sneaking in. But Olive, Peter, and even Lizzie just looked at her with confused expressions. She sighed and whispered, "Let's sneak in here."

"Ohhh," Olive and Peter said together. Lizzie gave her a thumbs-up. They slowly opened the back door and snuck into the shop. Each of them went a separate way, taking up different positions around the store. Beckett stood, talking to Ms. Henderson, at the counter near the back. Sarah caught a word here or there, but mostly she just heard a steady mumble as they talked. All four of them pretended to look at stuff whenever Ms. Henderson or Beckett moved their heads. When they weren't moving their heads, all four of them trained their eyes on him.

Suddenly, Beckett turned and moved toward the front door. Sarah cleared her throat and everyone immediately looked busy. But Lizzie was stuck at the front. She grabbed a newspaper from a rack by the door and raised it to cover her face. After Beckett went by, she slowly lowered the paper and caught Sarah's eye. Sarah knew Lizzie's look meant "CLOSE CALL." The newspaper was upside down.

Olive and Peter put down the 1950s bar glasses they'd both pretended to inspect and Sarah stepped out completely from behind a rack of old, fragile-looking dishes that made her nervous. The three of them moved toward the front door to talk to Lizzie. Sarah didn't think their cover had been blown. Or she hoped it hadn't, anyway.

Lizzie slumped in a chair near the front display window. "Ugh," she said. Sarah knew that meant "That was close! I need ice cream now." She just assumed the last part.

"Can I help you kids?" a voice behind them said. All four of them jumped. Lizzie clutched the paper so hard, it crumpled.

Sarah turned around and put on the smile she used for grown-ups. "No, thank you, Ms. Henderson." Weirdly, Annabelle Henderson would not answer to her first name, even though her store had it in the title. She'd always been a little eccentric. Besides the Regency dresses, there was a rumor that she used a chamber pot . . . but that always made Sarah and Lizzie collapse into giggles when they talked about it.

The shopkeeper smiled at Sarah. "I have your ice cream shop flyer up! Haven't gotten there myself yet, but I plan to. How has business been?"

Sarah said, "Oh, really good. Nothing at all bad has happened." Lizzie squeaked and Olive elbowed her. Peter smiled the fakest smile Sarah had ever seen. Sarah cleared her throat.

"Uh, Ms. Henderson, do you know the boy who just walked out?"

Ms. Henderson nodded. "Yes, that's Beckett. He goes to the private school just a town over."

Peter said, "What does 'a town over' mean?"

Sarah shot him a look and he shrugged and went on, "It's just, that's not really a measurement. . . ." But at the look on Sarah's face

AND the look on Olive's face, Peter stopped talking.

Sarah took a deep breath and continued. "Have you noticed that he's really . . . steal-y?"

Lizzie squeaked again and Sarah looked down. Maybe that wasn't the best way to put it, she realized.

Ms. Henderson furrowed her brow. "Um, steely? Do you mean having good resolve and a strong backbone? Indeed he does. He's a wonderful young man. He enjoys coming in here and looking for vintage reporter doodads. He likes those sorts of things. He also generously offered to help me with various and sundry tasks when I was unable to do them myself."

Olive pushed her glasses up. "Has he bought any really expensive things lately?"

Ms. Henderson laughed. "No, my dear, I don't think so. Not here, anyway. Not a whole lot that's expensive." She looked at them all suspiciously. "Why so many questions? In civilized cultures, one does not ask so many questions, my dears. Nor does one pry."

Lizzie got out of the chair. "Sorry, Ms. Henderson."

"Yeah, sorry," Sarah said, grabbing Lizzie's hand and pulling her out after her. Lizzie would get told what do to all day unless Sarah got her out of there. Lizzie grabbed Olive, who grabbed Peter, and they all beelined out of the store.

"Thanks, Ms. Henderson!" Sarah called. "I think my mom has something on hold for you at the library!" But by then the four had tripped through the front door and started running and giggling. Sarah, for just a second, forgot to be mad.

When they'd gotten well away from the store,

Sarah squinted and put her hand on her forehead to shield her eyes from the sun. It was so bright, she couldn't really see anything. She certainly didn't see Beckett. Her shoulders slumped.

"Did we lose him already? We JUST found him!" She huffed in frustration.

Peter said, "Didn't Ms. Henderson say he looked for reporter stuff in the store?"

Lizzie nodded. She was still holding the newspaper in her hands and was smoothing it down nervously.

"And?" Olive asked, pushing her glasses up and squinting at Peter.

"Maybe that's a clue to where he's going. Where do aspiring reporters go?"

Sarah had to admit that was really smart. But maybe not that helpful. But then Lizzie, looking to the left, said, "The coffee shop."

Olive pushed her glasses up again. Her nose looked as sweaty as Sarah's felt. Sarah really wished she was in the ice cream stand about now, with cold, delicious ice cream. She bet Lizzie was miserable in the heat.

"Why the coffee shop? Do reporters go there a lot?" Olive asked.

Lizzie pointed. "This one does."

And sure enough, through the window of Dinah's Diner (and Bait), Sarah saw Beckett in line. All four of them stared, not sure what to do next. But just then, he turned around and everything happened at once.

Lizzie squeaked and dropped to the ground. Sarah dove around Ms. Henderson's building into a patch of weeds. Olive said, "Oh, oh!" and did a sort of dance in place. And Peter just closed his eyes. They heard a bell jingle and Sarah watched as Beckett threw a confused look their way and then kept walking down Main Street.

Sarah got up and brushed the weeds off her knees. A dandelion was stuck to her skin and she plucked it off. She walked back to Lizzie and Peter and Olive. "Whoops . . . ," she said.

Olive looked distressed. "Do you think he saw us?"

Lizzie, Peter, and Sarah all looked at her. She cleared her throat and pushed her glasses up her nose. "Yeah, that's what I thought."

Peter said, "We should follow him—he's going into another store. This time that hardware store—and I think it sells bikes!" He pointed, and sure enough, Beckett had his coffee in one hand

and his other hand on the door of Hakeem's Hardware Plus Bait store. He opened it and walked in.

Lizzie said, "How will we . . ."

Sarah translated that to "He's totally going to see us."

"I have an idea," she said. "Why don't we take turns? Let's go to Dinah's Diner and ONE of us will follow Beckett, then come report to the others. Then switch off! Then maybe it won't be so obvious that we're watching him."

Olive grinned and Peter nodded. Sarah felt something grow in her. Was it . . . *like*? Did she actually LIKE Olive and Peter? So far they'd been pretty cool during the investigation. She eyed them, thinking.

But Lizzie interrupted her thoughts. "I don't think I can. . . . I don't want to. . . ."

Sarah knew immediately what she was talking about. She stepped in. "Someone else will go first."

And then she kind of understood what Olive meant. Maybe she and Lizzie DID have a special language.

But there was no time to think about it. Peter said, "I'll go."

"Okay," Olive said. "Peter, you go check out what he's doing in that hardware store. We'll go into the coffee shop."

They split up and the three girls walked to the coffee shop. When they got there, Sarah ordered a huge chocolate malt with whipped cream.

Dinah came over and gave everyone a hug. Rachel followed her with pastries for all of them. She said, "How are you liking our town, Olive?"

Olive, who had a malt too, smiled. "I like it a

lot. It's REALLY different from Boston, though. And I miss my friends."

Sarah felt a pang of guilt. She'd never even thought about having to leave her friends. What would she do if she had to leave Lizzie? Sarah suddenly felt like she understood a little better what her mom was talking about.

Rachel squeezed her shoulder. "Yes, most of us here moved from somewhere else. It's hard. But that's why we all stick together. And you're part of our family for as long as you're here!" Then she walked away.

Lizzie smiled at Olive, and Olive smiled back. Sarah tried not to feel jealous. Maybe she could just try to be better about all this.

Olive, Lizzie, and Sarah waited in the booth, on the lookout for Peter and their suspect. Sarah stared at the other stores on the street, trying to see everything as if it was all brand-new, all through Olive's and Peter's eyes.

Lizzie squeaked and pointed. Beckett was coming out of Hakeem's store, a small bag in his hand. A minute later, Peter followed. He saw them in Dinah's and jogged over.

Peter came into the shop, just a little breathless. He said, "Okay, here's the deal. He didn't buy anything big. Just an air pump. And he told the clerk he was going home. Do we know where he lives?"

Everyone looked at Lizzie. "What?" she said, alarmed. But then she looked away. She said quietly, "He lives on Plymouth Road in Hanoverville."

"Okay, let's go follow him," Sarah said. She got up and set her drink down.

"What about the plan to have just one of us

follow him?" Olive pushed her glasses up and squinted at Sarah.

"Well, if he's going home, I think we should confront him."

Lizzie squeaked, but Olive nodded slowly. "Yes. Get him on his home turf. Then maybe he'll feel comfortable enough to confess."

Peter nodded, and Lizzie just looked miserable. They all started discussing the pros and cons and walked out the door together. Sarah was saying to Lizzie, "It's really the best way, don't you think?" when everyone seemed to stop around her and Lizzie's face went pale.

Sarah looked up. Right at Beckett McIntyre.

"So why don't you four tell me why you're spying on me?" he said, taking a sip of his coffee.

CHAPTER 9

Vanilla Ice Cream. That's It.
No Hiding Anything.

U h," Lizzie said.

"Um . . . ," Peter said.

"What?" Olive and Sarah said in unison.

"Why are you spying on me? I saw you in Annabelle's, and then outside of Dinah's, doing some sort of weird group dance. Then this guy in Hakeem's. And now I overhear you saying you're going to follow me home. What gives?"

Sarah was impressed by how calm he was.

She didn't think she'd be that calm, that was for sure. But she knew the jig was up. She just hoped Lizzie had started breathing again.

Then Sarah realized something: they could have just been caught by a thief! So why was HE giving THEM a hard time? She put on a mean look.

"Let's go back inside, mister," Sarah said. "We have some questions for you." She put her hands on her hips and stared him down.

He shrugged. "Okay."

The five of them walked back in and Dinah said, "Your group keeps growing!"

Sarah mumbled under her breath, "Tell me about it."

They found a booth. Beckett sat on one side and the four of them scrunched in on the other,

Lizzie crammed against the wall, looking terrified and still clinging to the paper from Annabelle's. Sarah hung off the edge of the seat, keeping herself on it with no small effort of legwork. She tried to keep her look as mean as she could muster.

"We have some questions for YOU, Mr. Question-Asker," she said, her foot sliding so she almost fell off the bench. She scrunched into the booth more tightly and heard Lizzie grunt.

Beckett looked confused. "What are you talking about?"

Olive tried to lean forward, but she seemed stuck. "At the ice cream stand. You were asking us a bunch of questions."

"So?"

"So," Sarah continued, standing up—a choice

that was entirely her own and not because she couldn't keep her balance on the bench. "Better for intimidating thieves," she thought to herself. "So, you wanted to know all about how much money we made."

Beckett furrowed his brow. "Kind of. I mean, that was part of it."

Lizzie squeaked. Olive and Sarah said at the same time, "She means 'Why?'" Sarah stared at Olive. Olive shifted.

"Well, because I write for the newspaper. 'Kids' Corner'? I'm doing a story on your ice cream stand because it's run by four kids. I thought that was really cool. And the fact that you're trusted with so much money is super-cool too."

Sarah slumped back on the bench, practically in Olive's lap. Well. That made sense, unfortunately.

"Oh," said Olive and Peter at the same time.

Lizzie said, "See?"

Sarah said, "Dang."

Beckett leaned forward. "What is this all about? Are you upset I'm doing a story?"

Olive said, "We just lost—" but Sarah interrupted.

With a pasted-on smile, she said, "Gotcha! Ha ha! We just thought it would be funny to get your attention. So that you'll come back for the zombie hayride in the fall and write about it. So we can get more customers!"

Beckett furrowed his brow again. His look said, "You four are really strange. I need to leave." But what he said was "Okay. Good luck with everything! I will come back in the fall."

He got up and left, and Sarah slid around

to the other side of the booth, her shoulders slumped. Lizzie sighed dreamily.

Peter said, "Lizzie, check the paper you're holding to be sure."

Lizzie opened up the newspaper and smoothed it out. She looked at the table of contents and then turned to the "Kids' Corner" page. She pointed to his name. "There he is. And now he thinks we're a bunch of weirdos, following him around." She laid her head down on the paper.

Sarah patted her head. "I mean, at least he's coming back in the fall?"

Lizzie groaned. Peter said, "If we can find the money."

Sarah slumped in the booth even more. Everyone else seemed to deflate too.

Lizzie put her chin on her hand. "Sarah and her mom are coming over for dinner tonight. If we don't solve this today, we have to tell my parents."

Olive pushed a saltshaker with her finger. She shoved her glasses up. "Well, I want to suggest something, but I don't want to offend anyone."

Sarah thought, "That's a first," but she shrugged and waited. Lizzie nodded encouragingly.

Olive cleared her throat. "It's just . . . If Beckett didn't do it, then we have to consider other people. And the most likely people would be those who came to the ice cream stand."

Peter nodded. "Someone stole the money either because they needed it or because they didn't want us to have it."

Sarah had to admit that made sense. "So we

need to just think about every single person who's come to the stand?"

Olive and Peter nodded.

"Oh. Easy." Sarah snorted.

Lizzie said, "Well . . ." For once, Sarah had no idea what she meant. Lizzie went on, "We need to think about who came to the stand and if they said anything."

Sarah nodded, but a feeling of unease started in her stomach. She bounced her legs.

Lizzie put the newspaper on the table and asked if anyone had a pen. No one did, so Sarah grabbed one from the counter. When he came back, everyone looked at each other. Finally, Lizzie spoke. "Sarah, when we put up the flyers, lots of people weren't thrilled about a zombie hayride, remember?"

Sarah tapped her mouth with her finger. "Yeah. Stella didn't seem to like the idea. Or Rachel, come to think of it. But so what? Adults sometimes have wrong opinions. I've seen it a lot." She nodded sagely.

"Why didn't they like the idea?" Olive asked, pushing up her glasses again. Peter grabbed some toothpicks on the table and laid them out, putting them in different patterns. Sarah was mesmerized.

"What does it matter?" She eyed Olive suspiciously. "They would never DO anything about it."

Lizzie looked down at the table. She said, "Well . . . I remember someone saying all the shop owners here were losing money because business was slow."

Sarah whipped her head around to Lizzie. "So

you think they'd STEAL something from us?"

The four of them all looked at each other and then away. Sarah couldn't believe it.

Lizzie said, pleading with Sarah, "Sometimes good people do things because they're desperate. Or can only think of their own situation. You know, like in the old movies. Money makes people crazy."

Peter and Olive nodded gravely. "Like the one we watched together, *The Ukrainian Hawk*," Olive said. "The people weren't trying to be bad. They stole it to raise money to keep the town afloat."

Sarah huffed—why did they have to rub in the old movies all the time? But Lizzie might have a bit of a point. Money DID make people crazy. One time Sarah had accidentally used her mom's credit card to buy new shoes. Her mom didn't like that at all. Plus, Sarah had seen enough NEW movies to know it was true.

She made a decision. "Well, let's make a list," she said. "Just to prove they DIDN'T do it, okay?"

Lizzie nodded, looking relieved. "Yes! I don't think they would have done that either. But we should be thorough."

Peter and Olive nodded. "I'm sure they didn't. But we should just check to rule them out," Olive said. "They've been so nice to us. I don't want to think they did anything like that."

Sarah glared at her. "They didn't. We'll prove it. Let's split up and do some investigating. Uh, Peter and Olive in one group, me and Lizzie in another." She didn't look anyone in the eye and hoped hoped hoped they'd just go for it.

Peter said, "It might be faster if we all talked

to different people at the same time. We can get done quicker."

Sarah sighed. He wasn't wrong. Plus, that would get the people of the town off the hook sooner and let them figure out who the real culprit was.

"Fine," she said. "We have Rachel and Aaron, Hakeem, Stella, Ms. Henderson, Noa from Noa's Grocery and Bait, Mariko and Aldo . . . Anyone else, Lizzie?"

Lizzie thought for a second. "Sheriff Hadley wouldn't do it, since he's the law. . . ."

Sarah almost said, "DUH," but then she thought a little more. "I mean, I guess he was looking into going to a sci-fi conference? We should rule him out too." Lizzie nodded and wrote Sheriff Hadley's name down.

"But Dani didn't say anything, did she?" Lizzie asked.

Sarah shook her head. "None of the town would! But I don't think Dani needs the money; she has the town's money. And my mom wouldn't do it because she's my mom. And the library is funded by the state."

Olive and Peter were staring at them.

"What?" Sarah asked, wondering if she'd just sounded stupid.

"Do you know everyone in town? Like, every-one?" Peter asked.

Sarah shrugged. "Yeah."

Olive shook her head. "Wow. I can't even imagine."

Lizzie smiled. "Really, you do too now. I mean on Main Street, anyway."

"It's just so weird," Olive said. "In Boston, we only know certain people. And we'd call the police if our money got stolen. And . . . so many other things. Like, why does every store sell bait?" Olive scratched her head.

"Because we're near a lake, silly," Sarah said. DUH. But she didn't add that. She looked at the list and figured out quickly who should do what. "Anyway, if we're splitting up and doing this, here's what we'll do: Lizzie, you talk to Rachel, and Peter, you talk to Aaron. Then, when you're done, Lizzie, you talk to Stella, and Peter, you talk to Hakeem. Olive, you talk to Noa and then Mariko and Aldo. And I'll talk to the sheriff and to Ms. Henderson. Deal?"

Everyone nodded. Olive said, "Meet back here?"

Sarah shook her head. "No, let's meet back at the orchard. I don't want anyone to think we think they stole the money."

They all looked at each other seriously, then one by one left to get the town and its people off the hook.

CHAPTER 10

*Peach, Strawberry, and Spinach
Ice Cream. Or, Things That You May
Not Want but That You Need.*

Sarah decided to go see Sheriff Hadley first. She knew that he couldn't be the one who had taken the money, but she always liked talking to him. Even if he was really weird about her mom.

She opened the door to the sheriff's office and found him standing in front of a large half-painted blue box that was taller than him. He looked around the box when the door opened.

He had blue on his forehead, on his nose, and all over his fingers. His red hair stuck out all over and had blue streaks in it.

"Oh, hey there, Sarah," he said, then popped his head back around the box so she couldn't see him.

"I'm just painting a Tardis!" he said, his voice muffled. "I am going to leave it outside so people can come by and leave comments about the town and any improvements they think should happen. It'll seem a lot bigger on the inside, really."

Sarah walked over to the desk chair, which was behind the Tardis and the sheriff, and slumped in it, spinning it around with her legs. The blue was really pretty, but she had no idea what he was talking about. And she suddenly found herself feeling really grumpy.

Sheriff Hadley put the paintbrush down in the paint tray and grabbed a once-white towel now mostly covered in blue. He wiped his hands, but it only smeared the paint more evenly around them. Sarah stifled a giggle. Even as grumpy as she felt, that was funny.

"How are you doing, Sarah? And how is Ana?"

Sarah rolled her eyes. "My mom is fiiiiiiinnne," she said while spinning the chair around hard. The sheriff leaned against the wall.

"But something tells me you're not fine. Am I right?" He stared at her, one eyebrow up.

She shrugged. "I don't know. Maybe." She kicked her feet against the chair, suddenly, for no reason at all, feeling tears spring to her eyes.

He grabbed a folding chair that was leaning on the wall and sat on the other side of the desk, so that Sarah looked like the sheriff and he looked like a citizen. She smiled a little. But only a little.

"Well, Ms. Sarah, want to tell me what's going on? Sometimes sheriffs can be nice. Not always! But sometimes." He smiled at her and she shrugged again. But the left side of her mouth only went up into a half-smile.

She thought for a second. "Sheriff Hadley . . . let's say you like someone a lot. And they like you, too. But then one day other people come in and it seems like you don't count anymore. And the person you like seems to like the new people more, even though you've been together way longer—" She stopped. Sheriff Hadley's face had gone pale.

He said in a quiet, terrified voice, "Sarah, is your mom . . . Are you trying to tell me that your mom . . . Is your mom . . . dating someone?" He swallowed.

Sarah looked at the ceiling and made a sound of great irritation. "Uuuuuggghhh. No. Gross."

Sheriff Hadley ran his hand through his red hair and exhaled loudly. Then he said, "Oh, just kidding!" and gave the fakest laugh Sarah had ever heard. Except her own laugh when Mr. G told a bad dad joke. The sheriff went on, "Um, I think I know what you're saying, but do you want to say more?"

Sarah stared at her shoes and twirled her ankles. "I'm just afraid . . . Ugh. I think I might be losing my best friend."

Sheriff Hadley said softly, "Why do you think that?"

Two tears traveled down her face. She wiped

them away impatiently. "We don't like the same things a lot of times. We have a lot of fun together, but we're really different. And then . . . new people came and I think my best friend likes them better."

The sheriff chuckled. "I think I know who you're talking about. You don't need to talk in code."

"Fine. I think Lizzie isn't my best friend anymore because she likes Olive and Peter better." Two more tears streamed down her face—when she said it out loud like that, it made everything worse. She put her head down on Sheriff Hadley's desk and let the tears go. She felt him pat her hand, which was sticking out, and she let him do it. She sat back up and wiped her nose with her arm.

Sheriff Hadley said, "Ewwwwwww!" which made Sarah giggle hard. And then she got the giggles and couldn't stop laughing.

Finally, when she was done laughing, the sheriff looked at her seriously. "What did your mom say about it?"

Sarah looked him in the eye. "She said I should try to imagine what it's like to be Olive and Peter. Coming to this town and not knowing anyone. And that Nane and Papa had to come all the way over here from Iran and some people were mean to them. But many people were really nice. So . . . I guess that's what Lizzie is. She's the nice one."

Suddenly, something occurred to her. "Oh, no," she said. "Oh, no, Sheriff Hadley. I think that means I'm the . . . mean one!"

A wave of shame washed over her. She hadn't been nice to Olive and Peter at all. It wasn't their fault that she was worried about her friendship. And even if she was going to lose Lizzie, she couldn't be like the mean people who were terrible to Nane and Papa.

The sheriff spoke, again softly. "Listen, honey. You're not a mean person. You're working some things out. But if there's one thing I know and love about New Amity, it's that we take care of each other. We know what it's like to be on the outside. And so we make sure to let everybody in. And, my dear—you are a part of New Amity. There's always time to do the kind thing."

Sarah, with tears in her eyes for a different reason, nodded. "I have to go."

The sheriff smiled. "It sounds like it."

Sarah sprinted to the door and threw it open. She got about two steps away and then ran back inside.

Breathlessly, she said, "Sheriff Hadley, did you steal any money from the ice cream stand?"

The sheriff had his paintbrush in his hand again and popped around the almost-Tardis. "WHAT?" he said, his face twisted in confusion and already speckled with more blue.

Sarah yelled, "Didn't think so! Thanks, Sheriff Hadley!" and then she walked fast out the door again and started toward the orchard.

Then she stopped. She couldn't go back to the orchard yet, not without having talked to Ms. Henderson. She'd just have to stop there first. And anyway, she needed to think of what she'd say. Or how they could all make up. She started the walk to Annabelle's, thinking about the ways she'd make things better.

She imagined running up to Olive and Peter and saying, "WELCOME!" and then they'd hug her and laugh. And Olive would say, "Finally," and Peter would say something math-related or robot-related. And Lizzie would say to her, "You are the best person and friend anyone could ever hope to be." And then they'd have inside jokes among ALL of them and it would feel good for the first time since summer started.

Sarah hurried down the path, imagining all sorts of fun scenarios, and almost bulldozed right into Gloria.

"Excuse you, baby child. You should watch where you're going." Gloria wore a beret and sunglasses and a short red scarf tied around her neck. Her blue-striped shirt made her look like an old-fashioned sailor.

Sarah said, "Sorry, Gloria."

The chime on the door of Annabelle's tinkled, and Ms. Henderson stepped out. "Oh, goodness, I'm so glad I caught you. I found these for the props in the play. And I should have your costumes ready soon for you to try on. I've been working on them day and night all week—I haven't left this store or my apartment once!"

"Well, that means Ms. Henderson is out of the equation," thought Sarah. "That was easy."

Gloria looked over her sunglasses at the candlesticks Ms. Henderson had brought. "*Très magnifique*, Mademoiselle Henderson. I believe Nyo and Aisling will adore these as I do. *Bises!*" She leaned over and gave a surprised Ms. Henderson

167

a kiss on one cheek and then on the other. Now Sarah got it—Gloria was pretending to be French today.

Ms. Henderson beamed and said, "Good to see you again, Sarah. I hope you were all able to use the facilities after your visit today."

Sarah wrinkled her nose. "Huh?"

"Your potty dance outside the window. You had just left and then you all seemed to get a case of the . . . well, I won't say more. Already I fear I am indelicate. It is always good to see you." And with that she disappeared back into the store.

Sarah's face burned. Ms. Henderson was talking about when Beckett had seen them and they had each done something weird.

"Goodbye, baby child. I hope you needn't do a

pee-pee dance again." Gloria waved her hand and started down the path.

Sarah had a thought. She caught up with Gloria so they were walking side by side. "Gloria . . . how come you don't hang out with Jeff anymore?"

Gloria stopped abruptly. She fanned her face. "Oh, I'm afraid that topic is entirely too distressing. I shall not go into it." She started walking again, still fanning her face.

"Did you decide you liked Nyo and Aisling better? Is that what happened?" Sarah had to know. She had to.

Gloria stopped again. "How dare you, *mademoiselle*!" she said, then started walking yet again.

Sarah thought this might be an incredibly

long conversation. Gloria stopped again. Sarah also thought she might get whiplash from all the starts and stops.

"I'll tell you why we are not friends anymore! He decided not to support me in my new endeavors. Instead of being a GOOD friend, *très bien*, he chose to think my new life's passion was *stupide* and told me so. Then he stopped talking to ME. Can you believe it?" Gloria looked out into the distance, and for the first time, Sarah saw real hurt in her eyes.

"You think your best friend will support you no matter what. That he will grow with you instead of trying to hold on to only those things in the past. We didn't need to like the same things. He just had to understand that I liked them." Gloria sniffled and pushed her sunglasses back up. She continued, "It's no worry at this point. I've found people who do support me. All is *très bien* again." She began to walk fast away from Sarah. "Good-bye, baby child. *Au revoir!*"

This time Sarah let her go on ahead. She felt like she'd learned a lot, though. The bad part was—she'd learned a lot about herself. And maybe didn't like what she saw.

CHAPTER 11

No Ice Cream. Not Any.

*T*his time, Sarah would make it to the orchard, tell everyone what she knew, and . . . start again. This time, she'd be the kind of person everyone thought she was. The person she wanted to be. Suddenly, the zombie hayride and the stolen money didn't seem as important anymore.

Sarah ran back and got her bike from behind Annabelle's. It seemed like years since they'd followed Beckett. Well, at least Sarah felt older and wiser. No one else's bikes were there, and she was excited that everyone would be meeting at the orchard. She hopped on, mentally practicing things she was going to say when she caught up with everyone. She went back to her scenario, only made it bigger—more hugs! More of "You're so great, Sarah!" And from Lizzie? "I'm so happy you're my best friend." Sarah smiled to herself as she started biking toward Main Street.

She didn't get very far before she was stopped in her tracks. In front of Dinah's Diner (and Bait) were three bikes. Three bikes that should have been at the orchard. An uncomfortable feeling started in Sarah's stomach and traveled all the way to her head and all the way back to her feet. She got off her bike and walked it to the diner's window, dread making her steps heavy.

Sarah looked through the window—there Olive, Peter, and Lizzie sat in a booth. They were laughing hysterically and had gigantic malts in front of them again.

They were supposed to split up.

But instead, the three of them were using the time to have fun together—without Sarah.

Maybe they'd even planned it so that Sarah didn't ruin their fun with all her . . . Sarahness.

For the second time that day, tears sprang to her eyes. But this time, they were mad tears— mad tears at someone else. Sarah willed the tears away, sniffled, and let the mad feeling take over. She clenched her fists and huffed out her breath. Then, before her mom's voice could jump in and tell her to count to ten, she threw open the door and stormed into the diner. Right up to their table.

Lizzie's eyes got wide when she saw her. "Sarah . . . ," she said, but then stopped. Sarah wondered if Lizzie had no idea how to come clean that she'd betrayed Sarah so badly.

"I thought we were supposed to split up. But I guess *I* was just supposed to split up. I guess you all just wanted to hang out without me so you came up with this plan!" Sarah pointed to Peter. "You're the one who said we should split up." Then she pointed to Olive. "And YOU agreed." Then she looked at Lizzie. "I thought you were my best friend, Lizzie. But I guess I'm just a big old nuisance and you couldn't wait to get rid of me! I'm glad you found new friends and that you don't need me anymore! I hope you're all happy together!"

Sarah realized that the whole diner had gotten quiet. She hadn't really meant to make a scene. But then again, she was so upset, she didn't really care. Her whole life was falling apart—everything she'd thought she knew about her friendship and herself was totally wrong. Peter and Olive had ruined everything.

Before she started crying in front of everyone, Sarah ran out of the diner and grabbed her bike. She hopped on and rode harder than she ever had. She never wanted to see them ever again. The talks she'd had with Sheriff Hadley and Gloria seemed a million years away. Her worst fears were true—she didn't have her best friend anymore.

She pedaled all the way home, crying the whole time. When she got there, her mom saw her face and grabbed her in a big hug. "Oh, sweetie, I heard you had a bad day."

Sarah didn't even question it. News traveled fast in New Amity. And she'd just made a huge scene in front of everyone.

She let her mom take her to the couch and tuck her inside a blanket, even though it was a million degrees outside. Still, the air conditioning in their apartment was going hard and the room was nice and cool. The air made it feel to Sarah that the whole world was far, far away. Which was what she needed. For once, she was glad her mom wouldn't let her use a cell phone. Maybe it was good she didn't have to see texts from anyone. Or wonder what was being texted about her.

Her mom brought out some tea. Sarah took it, too miserable to say anything. Her mom patted her leg. "Want to talk about it?"

Sarah swallowed and shook her head. She didn't think she could start talking without crying. Her mom nodded and leaned back.

There was a knock on the door. Sarah's stomach clenched. She hoped above all else that it was Lizzie coming to tell her that she'd been wrong, that they were still best friends, and that she was sorry they'd left Sarah out. But Sarah also hoped it wasn't Lizzie. Sarah's mom went to the door, and Sarah listened closely as footsteps came down the hall.

Not Lizzie. The walk was all wrong.

Sheriff Hadley stuck his head into the living room and then the rest of him appeared. He still had blue all over himself. He was in the same white T-shirt and blue jeans he'd worn earlier, only he held his sheriff's hat in his hand.

"The sheriff is here to see you, honey. Colin, can I get you something to drink?" Sarah's mom touched her hair and pushed it away from her face. She touched her hair a lot around the sheriff. Her eyes got brighter too.

"Uh, that'd be great, Ana. I'll take some of that tea you make that's so delicious." He blushed and then shifted on his feet.

"Sure, Colin. Have a seat." They smiled at each other for what Sarah thought was a really weird amount of time.

Finally, her mom went into the kitchen and the sheriff sat down on a chair across from Sarah.

"It seems the plan you had after our talk earlier got derailed. You've had quite the day, huh?" he said, turning his hat in his hands and leaning forward.

Sarah nodded and rested her chin in her hand. She was so miserable, she didn't think she had any words left.

"You know, I happened to see Peter and Olive and Lizzie after you took off." Sarah's mom came back with the tea and set it down by the sheriff. "Thanks, Ana. I love your tea.

"You made quite the scene," the sheriff continued. Sarah looked down. "But mostly, all three of them were really upset that you were upset."

Sarah shrugged and mumbled, "Ghsroifish."

Sheriff Hadley said, "What, now?"

Sarah sighed. "I SAID, I was upset because they left me out on purpose."

The sheriff nodded for a second and then sat back, putting the hat on his knee. "Hmmm. Yeah, I can see how it looked like that."

Sarah played with the blanket on her lap.

"But, you know, in the training academy, they tell us that something like that is just circumstantial evidence. Do you know what that is?" he went on.

"DUH," Sarah said. Her mom squeezed her foot and Sarah knew that meant "Don't be rude." So she cleared her throat. "It means that the evidence could just LOOK one way, but it doesn't really prove anything."

Sheriff Hadley smiled. "Exactly. Smart as a whip, just like your mom." The sheriff and Sarah's mom smiled at each other. For way too long. Again.

"But that doesn't mean it's NOT right," said Sarah stubbornly. "Sometimes circumstantial evidence DOES point to something."

The sheriff nodded again. "That's true. One

of the best ways to get the right information, though, is to talk to people. Did you know that? It's amazing how truthful people can be when you just talk to them. My mom taught me that when she was sheriff."

Sarah didn't say anything.

"So after you left," he went on, "I just went up to those three and asked if they were okay. And they were just as upset as you. Because it seems like you didn't quite have all the information."

Now Sarah paid attention. She looked up.

Sheriff Hadley smiled and leaned forward again. "See, this is what they told me. They said you have some money missing from the safe—by the way, you could always come tell me, you know."

Sarah shrugged. She could feel her mom's eyes on her.

"But you can tell the Garrisons first before I get involved. Anyway, they told me the money was missing and you had all been doing your investigations. So you split up. But it became pretty clear to everyone fast that nothing was coming of it. So they went to Annabelle's to try to find you. I think you were interrogating me at that time." He stopped and looked at Sarah's mom. "A terrifying interrogator. We should use her for our crooks when we catch them."

Sarah played with the blanket but smiled a little.

"Anyway, they grabbed their bikes and then went to Dinah's to see if they couldn't catch you. And that way you could all ride together to the orchard."

Sarah looked up, her eyes huge. They were

trying to hang out with her? This made everything she'd said totally wrong. She swallowed. "They . . . they . . . were waiting for me?"

The sheriff nodded. "Oh, yes. They were coming up with a new idea. See, evidently, Peter and Olive offered to dip into their college fund to pay for the zombie hayride. They couldn't wait to tell you."

Sarah felt like she'd been kicked in the stomach. Her mom gave her a look that said, "Well, look what you did now, Sarah. See? Everyone loves you and you were just really mean."

Once again, Sarah had been the mean one. She needed some time to think things through. And they had the dinner tonight.

"I didn't . . . I didn't know" was what she ended up saying.

The sheriff nodded and then stood up, holding his hat. "I didn't think so, Sarah. You know what I said to them? I said, 'Sarah isn't normally like this. She's one of the best people I know.' And you know who agreed? Lizzie. She said she wasn't sure how to talk to you about this. That you don't seem to look at her anymore so it's hard to talk to you."

Now the tears trailed down Sarah's face. Lizzie was right.

But the sheriff wasn't done. "And you know who else agreed? Peter and Olive. Only, Olive said, 'We think she's great too. Though we wish she didn't hate us.'" He turned to Sarah's mom and said, "Ana, thanks so much for the tea. I'd love to . . . we should . . . I wonder if . . . Uh. Thanks so much for the tea."

Sarah's mom nodded and said, "Thanks for coming by, Sheriff. You're welcome anytime. Anytime. Stop by any, anytime." She walked with him to the front door, leaving Sarah feeling awful on the couch.

CHAPTER 12

Hot Fudge Sundae That Was TOO Hot but Is Now Cooled Down and with Some Toppings Might Sweeten Things a Bit?

Maybe I shouldn't go tonight," Sarah mumbled. The dinner was in just an hour and she didn't think she could feel any more awful. She didn't think she could face Peter and Olive. Not to mention Lizzie.

But her mom just said, "Would you like me to find you a book on making up? Maybe something by Stephen King . . . ," and went back to her closet to find something to wear, humming to herself.

Sometimes Sarah had a sneaking suspicion that her mom only pretended to be a space cadet. Just enough so that Sarah would have to figure things out for herself.

She got off the couch and washed her face. She changed into a shirt that Lizzie had gotten her—it said, OF ALL THE THINGS I'VE LOST IT'S MY MIND I MISS THE MOST. They had giggled for hours over it in a store, and Lizzie had bought it for Sarah for her birthday. Maybe the shirt would do two things: tell Lizzie she still wanted to be her friend and say that she knew she'd gone a little off the deep end.

"Ready?" Sarah's mom said.

Sarah swallowed, closed her eyes, and nodded.

She felt a peck on her forehead. "My little peanut butter nutter, sometimes the best thing you can do is face the music. Own up to what you did. Speak from the heart. You'd be amazed at what that can do."

Sarah nodded and, surprising even herself, took her mother's hand as they walked down the apartment stairs and to the car.

When they got to Lizzie's house, there was no Lizzie waiting on the porch. The house looked huge to Sarah, way huger than it had ever looked. And it seemed more shadowy, somehow. She dragged her feet as they got out of the car.

Normally she would have burst through the door, but everything was different now. Her mom rang the bell.

Mr. G answered. "Well, hello, Ana!" he yelled, looking cheery. "And Sarah! When we heard the doorbell, we expected a door-to-door salesman! Come in, come in!"

The house smelled delicious as always. Mr. G and Sarah's mom traipsed into the kitchen, leaving Sarah to linger by the stairs. She wondered if she should hit the banister three times—if she did it now, would it bring bad luck instead of good luck?

A voice in the living room spoke. "Aren't you going to hit the banister?" It was Lizzie. She walked into the light in the entranceway but stayed far away from Sarah.

Sarah shrugged. "I didn't want to ruin luck for everyone else," she said. Then she looked at the ground.

Lizzie didn't say anything for a minute.

Then she took a deep breath. "Peter and Olive quit the stand."

Sarah's head popped up. "What?"

Lizzie looked at Sarah with an unreadable expression. "They think they're causing too much trouble. So they quit."

Sarah wanted a hole to swallow her up. Before she could respond, Ms. G's booming voice announced dinner. Sarah began to say something, but Lizzie had already started walking to the table. Sarah had no choice but to follow.

Mr. G had made Sarah's favorite dinner: spaghetti and meatballs. Plus, there were hummus and pita appetizers, samosas with potatoes, spring rolls, and a Spanish omelet. He'd cooked enough for twenty people.

They all sat down, the adults talking animatedly and Sarah playing with her food. She couldn't taste anything, anyway. Plus, she and Lizzie had to tell them that the money was gone. Sarah wondered if the day could get any worse.

Lizzie's and Sarah's eyes met; Sarah knew that Lizzie knew it was time.

Lizzie cleared her throat. "Um . . . ," she said. But the adults kept talking. "Um . . . ," she tried again.

Sarah almost smiled. At least this was familiar. Only, it wasn't funny. Lizzie should be able to speak. "HEY!" Sarah practically yelled. "Lizzie has something to say."

Everyone stopped talking and looked at Sarah with surprise. Sarah caught a tiny smile on Lizzie's face and smiled back, just a little. A small, almost undetectable warm feeling started spreading through her.

"Uh, yeah," Lizzie said. "So, we lost all the money in the safe." She looked down at her plate.

Sarah couldn't stand to think that Lizzie felt bad. And she thought about Olive and Peter and how awful she'd been to them. So she sat up straight. "It was my fault. I'm sure I left the safe unlocked."

Lizzie gave her a questioning look. She was about to say something when Mr. G spoke up.

"Oh, no! It can't be too much, can it, though? I took the money to the bank around three thirty or so, and that left only a tiny bit of the day for you. I thought we should put that money in the bank since you're doing so well! But, are there extended hours for the stand now? Hmm. Did you make that decision, Tabitha? That might not be a great idea, although if they're already making so much money, then this is a big deal, wow! Also, that might be against the law, work-wise . . ."

"Dad," Lizzie said loudly. She shrank back a little from the sound of her own voice, but Sarah got a zing of pride watching her take center stage. She cleared her throat. "Are you saying you took the money from the safe while we were working?"

Mr. G nodded. "Oh, yes. Didn't you get my note?"

Sarah could hardly believe her ears. She felt like she was going to fall over with relief. Lizzie put her head in her hands. Her shoulders were shaking. At first Sarah thought she was crying, but then she saw that she was laughing. This made Sarah start too. The laugh began in her toes and came all the way up to her stomach, making her hold it to keep it from falling apart.

"Mr. G," Sarah said through guffaws, "I think you forgot to leave the note."

Mr. G said, "Oh, no! I'm positive I did. Because I used this little pencil here"—he rummaged around in his pocket—"that I found on the ground outside and I thought, 'I wonder if we put together all the pencils that were lost somewhere end to end, how many times would it encircle the Earth—'" He stopped abruptly as he pulled up the pencil. Because with it was a crumpled piece of paper.

He opened the note and read it, then put it back in his pocket. "Whoops." He smiled and shrugged. "Guess I didn't leave it there! I hope that didn't worry you."

The more she thought about it, the more Sarah could not stop laughing. She thought about the past couple of days. And then everything that'd happened just that very day. They'd spent all day following some poor, unsuspecting kid because they thought he'd been stealing. And they didn't even do a good job of trailing him! He'd figured it out long before *they* figured out how to do it in a way that he wouldn't notice. They must have looked so silly.

Sarah's laughs got bigger and bigger, until she was, much to her embarrassment, snorting. Loudly. She couldn't stop. "I'm just . . . thinking about the antiques store . . . and outside . . . when I dove into weeds and Olive . . . and Lizzie . . ." She honestly couldn't breathe.

Lizzie was now helplessly laughing too. She

held her stomach and leaned over. "And . . . and . . . then we thought everybody in town stole . . ." This made Sarah start another round of laughing. She even hit the table a few times, making the spaghetti jump. When Sarah got ahold of herself, she managed to look up and see all three adults staring at her and Lizzie, dumbfounded.

Sarah wiped her eyes and took a deep breath. She looked at Lizzie. It was time. "Lizzie, can I talk to you?"

Lizzie wiped her eyes too and nodded.

"May we be excused?" Sarah asked her mom and the Garrisons. They all looked at each other and shrugged, as if they'd planned it.

Sarah and Lizzie, without having to say anything out loud, walked through the kitchen and through the back door to the gazebo in back.

The Garrisons had lit it with tiny white lights and had put mosquito netting around it. It was one of Sarah's favorite places. There was a swing in there and a comfy chair. Sarah took the swing and Lizzie sat on the chair.

The only sounds were the crickets, which were getting loud. The sun was just setting, and Sarah thought she might actually think it was super-pretty, if she didn't have to talk about how mean she'd been.

"Lizzie, I'm so sorry. I've been awful. I was so mean to Peter and Olive and it was for stupid reasons. I don't know why I acted like that." Although, really, she did.

Lizzie sat cross-legged and put her chin on her hands. "I don't understand, Sarah. You're normally the one who takes people in. Or, at least, fights for them. Remember in first grade when we cornered Tom Patel and told him he couldn't pick on people anymore? You always help people who are getting picked on." And here Lizzie started crying. "But this time, I watched you, my best friend, start picking on people who were just trying to be nice and to fit in. And I knew you were hurting, but I couldn't help."

Sarah swung furiously, trying not to cry, but it didn't work. It was worse that Lizzie was disappointed in her. Way worse.

Sarah said through tears, "I know. I just . . . I got scared, Lizzie." And then everything came pouring out. "Because it seemed like you had so much in common with Peter and Olive. And Gloria and her best friend just STOPPED being friends one day. So I was afraid that would happen to us! I don't like old movies—and you don't like sports or math. What if the only thing we had in common was the zombie hayride? And then Peter and Olive came along and you did your voices with them and Olive finished your sentences and they liked the zombie hayride too so it wasn't just ours anymore and then they got to be in the ice cream stand too and then THAT wasn't just ours anymore and I thought you were going to be like Gloria and not be friends with me anymore and I don't know what I'd do if that happened, Lizzie. Because you are my best friend always and I will never not want you to be." Sarah finished with a huge sob. All the stress of the past two weeks, all of the feeling left out, and the worry, and all of the disappointment in herself, came rushing through a flood of tears. She buried her head in her hands.

She felt the swing move and then arms wrap around her. Lizzie was bear-hugging her and crying too.

"Mmgsdfffatowt," Lizzie said.

Sarah said, "What?" and then sniffed so loudly, it startled Lizzie. They both giggled and sat back.

Lizzie said, "I am ALWAYS your best friend. I don't care if you don't like the exact same things I do. How boring would that be? I just want you to be you. You NEVER have to worry about that." Her eyes teared up again. "I can't believe you thought that."

Sarah laughed. "Well, now it seems silly."

In a British accent, Lizzie said, "Quite right, good fellow!" And then they were off snort-laughing again.

It felt good. The warm fuzzy feeling was back—Sarah felt like she could fly. She had her best friend back.

She had actually never lost her.

But there was still work to do. There were two more people she needed to make amends to. And she wanted more than ever to really be their friends.

"Lizzie, I really want to make it up to Peter and Olive. I have been so terrible to them, and you know what? I think I would really like them." Lizzie nodded so hard, her head almost bumped up against the back of the swing.

"So I need to come up with some way, some big gesture to make sure they know they're welcome here. . . ." Sarah looked out of the gazebo and tapped her finger on her mouth.

Lizzie's eyes sparkled. "I think I have an idea. Can you stand watching some old movies?"

Sarah grinned. "I can stand anything as long as you're my best friend and I get two NEW best friends soon too!"

Lizzie squeaked and then said, "Deal. Follow me."

CHAPTER 13

Mint Chocolate Chip Ice Cream, Plus All the Toppings, Plus Swedish Fish, Equals Please Come Back to the Stand

Sarah yawned. It was after midnight and she and Lizzie had been watching movies for hours. But they had finally come up with a game plan and Sarah was excited, as well as exhausted.

Lizzie blinked at her sleepily. "So, tomorrow we do some supercuts? I think Gloria could help."

Sarah groaned and rolled her eyes and put on her best Gloria voice, which wasn't that great.

"Dear babies, why is it you cut up movies?"

Lizzie giggled and in a Gloria voice that was that great said, "Why do you bother me with such baby things? ACTING!"

Sarah yelled, "ACTING!" And then they collapsed in giggles. Sarah settled into her sleeping bag in Lizzie's room. Lizzie was on the floor in her sleeping bag too, even though she had her bed right there. But they both liked to sleep in the bags on the floor, even though the floor was a little drafty in the old house. Still, this was what they always did. Though Sarah thought they could probably come up with something different soon—and it would be okay.

Lizzie fell asleep almost immediately, but Sarah was still thinking hard about things. She was nervous about tomorrow. The stand opened at eleven. She had to put all these clips together, and Lizzie had to talk Peter and Olive into coming to the orchard beforehand. She hoped against hope it wasn't too late to make things better.

The next morning was a blur of activity. The first thing they had to do was wake up Gloria. Lizzie tiptoed into her room and Sarah stood by the door. Gloria had remodeled her room with huge, fancy curtains and had even made a paper chandelier and had put it over the light fixture up above. She slept with an eye mask on.

Lizzie gently shook her. "Gloria," she whispered. "Wake up, Gloria." Gloria grunted and rolled over, and Sarah thought she saw some drool. Gross. "Gloria . . . ," Lizzie gently said.

Suddenly, Gloria sat straight up and said, "Stanislavski!" Lizzie looked back at Sarah with bewilderment. Sarah shrugged. She'd long ago stopped trying to make sense out of Gloria.

Lizzie cleared her throat. "I'm sorry to wake you up, Gloria. But we need your help."

Gloria blinked at her.

Lizzie went on, "I mean, you're the ONLY one who can help us. Can you come to the office?"

Gloria blinked some more. Finally, she said, "I will help you, as I am the only one who can." Lizzie turned to Sarah and gave her a thumbs-up. While she was doing that, Gloria went back to sleep.

Ms. G appeared next to Sarah, a coffee cup in her hand. She put her hand on Sarah's shoulder and said, "Oh, Lizzie. You know getting her up before twelve o'clock is useless. Can I help with something?"

Gloria had already begun to snore again.

Lizzie sighed and joined Sarah and Ms. G in the hallway, shutting Gloria's door behind her.

"We need to splice some movie clips together," Lizzie said.

Sarah nodded. "I'm trying to apologize to Peter and Olive. And we figured out how to do everything except put all the clips of the movies together."

Ms. G enveloped Sarah in a hug. Sarah leaned into it. "That's wonderful. And as a matter of fact, I CAN help with that. I've been working on some home movie stuff myself. Let's get going."

Sarah looked at Lizzie. "Are you going to call Peter and Olive?"

Lizzie nodded. "I'm going to help Dad out for a little bit, and then I'll call. It's only seven o'clock. I don't want to wake them. I want them in the best mood when we talk." She crossed her fingers. Sarah crossed her fingers too. Then Lizzie went to help her dad, and Sarah and Ms. G went to the office.

Two hours later, Sarah and Ms. G high-fived. They had spliced all the movies together and made an AMAZING supercut.

Lizzie came in almost at the exact moment they finished. She looked a little down. But she smiled at Sarah anyway. "Guess what?" she said.

Sarah's stomach flipped. This had to be about Peter and Olive. "Did they . . ."

"YES!" said Lizzie. Sarah got up and grabbed

Lizzie's arms and they both jumped up and down, squealing.

Ms. G laughed and got up, stretching. "Well, I'll leave you two to it."

"Thanks, Ms. G," Sarah said.

Ms. G put her hand on Sarah's head and said, "You're doing the right thing. I'm proud of you. And your mother is too."

Sarah got a little teary but pushed the tears back. Now wasn't the time.

"Should we make the flyers?" Lizzie asked.

Sarah nodded and grinned. "Definitely."

At ten o'clock, Sarah stood near the counter in the ice cream stand, nervous and pacing. Lizzie was there too, chewing on her fingers. The stand was decorated with all sorts of glittery flyers and a huge homemade sign that said WELCOME on it. The TV/DVD combo they'd borrowed from Lizzie's parents stood next to the cash register. Sarah was going to do this right. Now they just needed Peter and Olive to follow the signs and flags that she and Lizzie had planted all the way from Lizzie's house to the stand.

If everything went well, they should be there any moment.

Lizzie suddenly squeaked. Sarah knew that meant they were on their way. She and Lizzie ducked behind the counter and peeked over it.

Olive and Peter came walking up, their faces full of confusion. They read the sign that said WELCOME, and then Olive said to Peter, "Are you sure those signs were for us?"

Sarah took the remote control for the TV/ DVD combination and pressed Play.

The movie Sarah and Lizzie had put together started playing.

It started out with a clip from a movie that said, "Welcome!" and went on from there. Sarah and Lizzie had picked parts from twelve old movies. They'd put them together to say:

"Welcome! I am so glad you're here. I am so sorry I was a rapscallion. A scallywag. A hooligan. A ne'er-do-well. A two-faced bucket of howdy-doody.

"I really like you. Please, can we be friends?

"Also, ZOMBIES!"

The last clip was from a black-and-white movie with zombies ambling toward people. At that, Sarah jumped up from behind the counter and did her zombie impression. Lizzie was supposed to too, but she didn't move right away. When she did, her eyes were bright and shiny, but she groaned and walked like a zombie.

"Brrraaaaiiinnnns," Sarah said. Then she went into the back of the ice cream stand, went out the door, and walked to Peter and Olive, who were standing near the counter, facing the stand. Lizzie stood near her.

Peter and Olive were laughing. Olive pushed her glasses back up her nose and said, "That was amazing!"

Sarah swallowed and got serious. "I am really sorry I've been so awful. I was afraid I was losing Lizzie as a friend and I acted . . . bad. I am so glad you're here. I really like you guys! Will you still work the stand with us? And . . ." Sarah looked down. "And maybe consider being my friend?"

For a second, nobody moved. And then Olive threw her arms around Sarah, and Peter did too. And then Lizzie threw her arms around all of them.

It was exactly how Sarah had imagined it.

When they split up, Peter said, "You put all this together for us?"

Sarah nodded. "I mean, it was the least I could do! And I plan on making this up to you all summer! And THEN. When we plan the zombie hayride, too!"

Peter high-fived Olive and then Sarah. He put his hand out to Lizzie, but she sniffled and looked down.

Sarah had a terrible thought—was LIZZIE jealous now?

But it was Lizzie, and Sarah didn't think she had it in her. "What's going on, Lizzie?"

Lizzie looked up and tears shone in her eyes. "I hate to ruin this moment, but . . . you should all probably know. This morning, our tractor broke. It's been acting up and they've been getting it fixed over and over. But this time, it can't be fixed. So any money we get from the stand HAS to go to a new tractor. Otherwise the orchard could go out of business if we can't grow, you know, apples."

The news hit them like an ice cream cone splatting on a sidewalk. Sarah slumped against the stand. Peter looked up and huffed out his breath. And Olive put her face in her hands and shook her head.

Sarah realized: this hayride wasn't just important to her and Lizzie. It was important to Peter and Olive, too.

It was their thing. The four of them. A symbol of ALL of their friendship. She racked her brains to come up with some solution.

When she looked up, she saw a slow smile start on Peter's face. "MOO!" he said.

Sarah and Lizzie exchanged confused glances. And even Olive joined in, sharing the same confused look with them.

"MOO!" Peter said again, clapping his hands together triumphantly.

"Um, we don't have . . . ," Lizzie started.

"Cows," Olive and Sarah finished. Then they all smiled at each other.

Peter grinned wider. "No, remember that contest flyer thing? Isn't there an ice cream contest we can enter? And get the EXACT AMOUNT OF MONEY we need if our sundae wins?"

Sarah felt her eyes grow wide. He was right. She hadn't even thought about the flyer since they'd first seen it—they'd been too busy and too sure they would make enough money. But if they could make the best sundae and win the contest . . .

Lizzie squeaked.

"Peter, you're brilliant!" Sarah crowed. "Okay, so when is the contest?"

"I thought it said at the end of June? So in like a week?" Olive said. Peter and Lizzie nodded.

"Well, then, this might just work! In the next week, let's create the best sundae Moo has ever tasted. I think with the four of us, we can figure this out?" Sarah said, determination zinging through her. "Are we all together on this?" she asked.

She looked at Lizzie, who nodded.

She looked at Olive, who smiled and said, "Oh, heck yes."

And she looked at Peter, who said, "Let's do this."

Sarah smiled. They were going to do this.

CHAPTER 14

Red Licorice Bits with Raspberry Vanilla Ice Cream and Other Sweet, Sweet Things That Will Make Everything Better

O kay, where do we start?" Sarah asked, still smiling. No one said anything. They all just looked at one another.

"The stand opens in a half hour. Maybe we should think about it and come back tomorrow with ideas?" Olive said, pushing up her glasses.

Sarah nodded. "Yeah, that might be the best idea. . . ."

Lizzie shrugged and Peter moved to the

stand. They had a shift to do. And a lot of think-ing, it turned out.

They all went to the back of the stand and put on their aprons. Sarah felt a little shy—she'd spent so much time not liking them, she didn't know how to just be normal. So she started with questions. That was what her mom would say she should do.

"Peter, you really like math, huh?" she said, taking ice cream out of the freezer.

He nodded. "Yeah."

Sarah said, "Me too! Lizzie doesn't like it, though."

Lizzie shook her head. Olive laughed. "Me nei-ther. I like science the best. And art. Like my dad."

Peter got out a few toppings and Lizzie got

some out too. Olive grabbed scoops and napkin refills.

Sarah said, "Did you say you build robots, too?"

Peter nodded. "Yeah, but Olive helps. She's good at that, too."

"I always wanted a brother or sister," Sarah said. "Is it cool being twins?"

Lizzie looked at her funny. "Really? I didn't know you always wanted a sibling." Sarah shrugged. Then Lizzie smiled. "You can take mine!" she said, and everybody laughed.

Peter said, "Being twins is cool. Olive is my best friend. But sometimes it's hard to go out and make other friends, because you don't really need them. So . . ." He stopped and smiled big.

"This whole new-friend thing is also pretty cool. We have friends in Boston, but everyone is always so busy, to be honest, sometimes it's hard to even hang out."

Sarah smiled at him. "Just wait until we get to figure out the zombie hayride together!"

Lizzie's face turned to worry. "We have to win that contest first," she said.

Sarah nodded. Before, she'd wanted the hayride to make sure she and Lizzie had something in common. But now she wanted it to give her new friends something fun to do with them, all together.

The bell chimed outside, meaning their first customer was here. Sarah realized they had all worked together without having to figure out who did what. Like they'd been a group of friends forever. She smiled, thinking about that. It felt pretty good.

When Sarah got home, she was exhausted. And still at a loss as to how to figure out the best sundae. She knew what SHE liked . . . but did that mean other people would like that too? She doubted it.

At dinner, her mom kept talking about a new book that had come in and the way she'd get to expand the children's section. Sarah thought that was all well and good, but she was practically an adult so it didn't really affect her. She stared off into space and barely touched her tacos.

"Okay, kitten pie, is everything okay? Didn't

you and Lizzie have a good time last night? It seemed like things were good."

Sarah snapped back to the present. "Oh, they are! Things are way better." She recapped for her mom all the things that had happened that day—the movie clips, the making up, the news about the stand, and the contest.

Her mom beamed with delight. "I need to tell Colin that his advice worked! And I'm so proud of you, honey. That was really mature of you. I just wish the hayride had worked out."

Sarah bristled. "It still might! We just have to come up with the best sundae ever. . . ." Saying it out loud made her immediately cranky.

Her mom noticed. "You know, sometimes the best thing to do to solve a problem is to forget it for a while." Sarah huffed. She highly doubted that. But her mom went on, "I'm serious. I know what I'm talking about. So, how about this, peanut butter nutter? Let's finish dinner and go watch some mindless TV. I think I saw that *X-Men* was on. What do you think?"

Sarah couldn't pass that up. She nodded and took a bite of her taco. Her mom hardly ever let her watch TV. In their house, it was always about reading. Plus, *X-Men* was Sarah's FAVORITE. She always wondered what her mutant power would be.

She finished her tacos fast, her mom laughing at her as she chomped through the hard shell and made everything fall out. Sarah giggled too, but the giggling did not stop her taco annihilation. She and her mom did the dishes, and then Sarah practically ran out and slid onto the couch, grabbing the remote along the way and flipping to the guide.

Her mom ambled in while Sarah tried to find the channel *X-Men* would be on. "Oh, it's channel forty-five. And we have perfect timing. It starts in about five minutes." Sarah turned to the right channel and then snuggled into the couch. Her mom set a drink down and settled into the couch too. She squeezed Sarah's foot. "A perfect night!"

About twenty commercials came on and Sarah bounced her legs. Why did everything take so long? But her mom said, "Ooh, I love this commercial," when the screen changed to a stylish scene with perfect-looking people.

The commercial was about a family coming together to eat dinner, parents, grandparents, a bunch of kids, and a cute dog. They'd been fighting, and everyone had had a bad day, but sitting at the table, they listened to each other. At the end of the commercial, a voice said, "Box and Bundle. We bring family together."

Sarah looked at her mom. Tears were streaming down her face and she hiccupped. She saw Sarah looking at her and she laughed a little. "I know it's silly, but they were fighting and then they were getting along and they remembered they loved each other as a family! This commercial always makes me cry." Sarah's mom grabbed a tissue and blew her nose loudly, and Sarah scrunched her face up.

"Mom, it's a commercial for a place we never even go to."

Her mom wiped her nose and then dried her eyes. "Oh, I know, honey. But you can bet the next time we go into the city, we'll go there. The story they tell is what reels customers in." She winked at Sarah and then said, "Is it too soon to have popcorn?" She got up before Sarah could answer, muttering, "Families . . . coming together . . ."

Slowly, something dawned on Sarah. A grin lit up her face. When her mom came back in, she looked at Sarah suspiciously.

"Did you just put a whoopee cushion down or something? Why are you smiling so big?"

Sarah laughed. "Oh, nothing. I think you just solved my problem, that's all."

Her mom shrugged. "Well. I think we figured out my mutant power." She tweaked Sarah's nose and sat down. "See? I told you that you just needed to put it aside!"

Sarah totally agreed.

♡

The next day, Sarah asked everyone to meet her at the ice cream stand early, before their shift. They gathered around the freezers and all looked at her expectantly.

"Right. So. I have an idea. Last night my mom cried at a commercial," she said.

Olive nodded. "My dad cries at commercials all the time."

Peter grinned. "Yeah, especially that one . . . What is that one, Olive?"

Olive said, "It's a new one about that place that sells plates. . . ."

Sarah pointed excitedly. "Yes! That's the same one my mom cries at! Last night we were going to watch *X-Men* and then this commercial came on and she started crying because the story was so moving. It makes her cry every time, she said. And she also said she would definitely go to the plate place now."

Lizzie said, "Yeah . . . ?" Sarah knew that meant "What's your point?" So she got to it quickly.

"My mom said the story sells the product," she said. "And we have a good story."

Lizzie, Olive, and Peter all looked at each other, then at Sarah. Olive asked, "What story?"

Sarah beamed. "We have the story of us! We're like the *X-Men*! Each of us brings something good to our group, and when we combine all our ingredients together, we get the best mix of things ever!"

A slow smile spread over Lizzie's face. Olive and Peter started smiling too.

"So let's spend today thinking of our favorite things, and then after our shift, we can put them together. I'm going to guess it will make the best sundae ever. Then, when we take it to MOO, we tell them all about our story. And what makes our group of friends special! What do you think?"

Lizzie nodded big. Peter and Olive smiled and nodded too. Sarah couldn't WAIT until the end of the day.

CHAPTER 15

Four Different Flavors Plus Lots of Toppings Equals a WINNING Combination

Olive looked down her nose at Sarah while pushing her glasses up. Sarah was beginning to think of it as Olive's signature move. Two weeks ago it would have driven her crazy; now it made her smile.

Olive pointed to Sarah's bouncing knee. "You're going to bounce your leg off, you're doing it so hard."

Sarah swallowed and tried to stop bouncing.

She had a bad habit of fidgeting and moving when she was nervous—and she hadn't been this nervous in a long, long time. She was pretty sure she'd go through the roof soon if they weren't called in.

The four of them sat outside the room where the judges were. They'd been waiting for more than two hours. Peter had stood up to investigate MOO posters around the room, staring at each of them as if they had an interesting code to break. Lizzie was playing with the ends of her hair, twisting strands and then watching them bounce back up when she let go. Olive kept taking deep breaths and then sighing. Sarah wished her mom could have come. But she was at the library, getting interviewed about her program with kids for the summer. Sarah couldn't be too mad at her. She was excited about it, so Sarah had to support her. If there was one thing she'd learned this summer, it was that supporting the people she cared about was important.

Mr. G was the one who had taken them all to Boston to show their creation. They'd driven up that morning, put their masterpiece in the large freezer that held everyone else's, too, and come to the waiting room.

Where Sarah was pretty much bouncing off the ceiling.

"Uh, the Apple Orchard Crew?" a voice said. Sarah looked up. Someone with a clipboard and a walkie-talkie stood by the door to the room with the judges. Sarah swallowed and looked at Lizzie. Lizzie's eyes were huge and she made a gurgling sound. Sarah felt the same way. If she said that out loud, it would sound like "Holy schmolies it's now or never oh my gosh it's our turn to go what if I don't say things right and we lose everything because of me?" Or something like that. Sarah was having a hard time translating, since she could barely translate her own thoughts.

"Go get 'em, guys!" Mr. G said. "I'll be in the back watching, okay?" Sarah nodded numbly, and then all four of them got up. The walk to the place in front of the judges was the longest walk Sarah had ever taken.

Finally, Sarah, Olive, Peter, and Lizzie stood in front of the three judges. Their creation sat in front of them, big and beautiful. Sarah could feel herself start to relax. They'd made a really cool sundae. Now they just needed to explain why.

"Hello, contestants," said one of the judges, a dark-haired woman with kind eyes. "I do think you are the youngest contestants we have!" She smiled at each one of them.

The woman in the middle, who seemed very business-y, said, "Yes, you are the youngest. What do you have for us today?" The other judge, a man who looked a lot like Mr. Garrison, stayed silent.

Sarah cleared her throat. It was now or never. If they could just convince the judges that they deserved to win. They'd worked hard and worked together. The way friends did.

She began. "Um, hi. So, we want to intro-duce ourselves and tell you about us. Because we think we made something special here, because each of us is special."

Olive jumped in as they'd practiced. "And

when you put us all together, you get something extraordinary."

Peter said, "It might seem like these things don't go together."

And Lizzie finished the introduction: "But we found out that the best sundae of all is one that includes flavors and toppings that bring out the best in the rest of the sundae."

Sarah took over. She pointed to Lizzie. "This is Lizzie. Her family has owned an apple orchard for at least two hundred years. And Lizzie and I have been friends since we were babies. See, the orchard has always been a home to me, and Lizzie has always been my best friend. And this year, we got to be in charge of the ice cream stand, but only because Lizzie's sister and her best friend had a falling-out. And then we got some good news: if we made enough money, then we could make a zombie hayride for the fall. I couldn't wait! Because I was afraid that Lizzie and I would have a falling-out like her sister and her best friend. And zombies were something we loved together." She looked at Peter and Olive and smiled at them. "But then Olive and Peter came, and at the beginning, I thought they'd ruined everything."

Lizzie picked up the story. "Sarah has always been really kind to others and has always made sure people are nice to each other. She's beaten people up because of it!" Sarah saw one of the judges smile and look down. "But all of a sudden, she started acting funny. I couldn't understand why she was acting like that and it hurt me to see her hurt. And to see her be different than how I know she is. Especially because Peter and Olive are so great! I didn't know she was worried about our friendship. She let that take over everything and she was missing out on making two new friends. And being mean to them in the process."

Olive continued: "Peter and I are here because our dad is on a sabbatical and doing a study of the orchard and our other dad is going to work on sculptures. We were SO NERVOUS to leave everything here in Boston and go to such a small town. We knew we wouldn't know anyone. We'd miss our friends and all the stuff we like to do in Boston. We would have to go to a new school in the fall. So when our dads came in and said they'd met the orchard people and that there were kids for us to meet and hang out with all summer, we were really excited. But then we met Sarah and Lizzie, and it seemed like they didn't want us there. Or like Sarah didn't, anyway."

Peter went on, "I don't talk a lot. And with Sarah I didn't talk at all."

Sarah jumped in. "But then my mom talked to me about being good to people who are new, because it's hard. My mom's parents were new to America, and they met not-nice people and nice people. So then I realized I was being a not-nice person. That I was letting my fears take over, like my mom would have said. And most of all that I wasn't losing Lizzie—I was gaining two awesome new friends." She looked at them and smiled, a real, big, goofy smile. "Together we make a really good team. We may be different, or not like the same things, but when you put everything all together . . ."

Lizzie, Olive, Peter, and Sarah said at the same time, as they'd practiced over and over: "YOU GET SOMETHING AWESOME."

The judges all smiled, and Sarah thought she heard Mr. G sniff in the back. She had to admit, even she felt a little emotional, and it was her own story!

Lizzie said, "So, in this sundae, you have one tower of real vanilla ice cream topped with cookie crumbles."

Olive said, "And one tower of Neapolitan ice cream with candied almonds on top."

Peter said, "And one tower of eight different ice creams topped with Swedish Fish."

Sarah said, "And one tower of bubble gum

ice cream with gummy worms and Skittles."

"All covered in whipped cream," Olive said, smiling big.

"Yep!" said Lizzie. "We all agreed on the whipped cream."

"And the cherry on top," Peter said.

"But wait! There's more!" Sarah went up to the creation and turned the plate toward her. There the button that Peter and Olive had planted showed. Sarah pushed it and waited.

For a second, nothing happened. Then chocolate syrup started coming up through the middle of all the towers and flowing over.

Peter beamed. "We made a volcano mechanism for this. So this is molten fudge!"

The judges all laughed. Sarah turned off the button so the fudge wouldn't drip over the plate.

"And what do you call this creation?" the judge with the kind eyes asked.

Sarah looked at Olive and nodded. Olive said, "We call it 'Ice Cream Summers Make the Best Friends.'"

All three judges looked confused. But this only made Sarah, Lizzie, Olive, and Peter all crack up. They knew it was a silly name. But it was a silly name that described their creation perfectly.

They all high-fived each other, still laughing.

The no-nonsense judge said, "We'll let you know in the next couple of days whether or not you've won."

"Thank you!" Lizzie, Peter, Olive, and Sarah all said at the same time, making them break out into fresh giggles.

Sarah had no idea if they even had a chance of winning. But she did know that she now had two new friends she couldn't imagine summer without. And that was the best creation of all.

CHAPTER 16

All the Flavors in the World Can't Compare to Living in New Amity

One week later, Lizzie, Sarah, Olive, and Peter sat in the ice cream stand on break. They'd heard back from **MOO** and found out they had not won. Not even second place. Sarah was a little disappointed, but not surprised. She was sad about the zombie hayride, but it didn't feel so important anymore. Plus, they still got to eat ice cream all summer. That was cool. At least that was what she kept telling herself.

The morning had been completely dead, which wasn't totally surprising. It was Sunday morning and a lot of people were at the town hall for Community Spirit. Most everyone in the town went there to share good news and heartaches, to support each other, and to find things they were grateful for.

At exactly twelve o'clock, the bell they put out in front of the ice cream stand at lunchtime started dinging and Sarah startled. Community Spirit must be over. Sarah was glad they'd be busier now. Even though no one was surprised they'd lost, Sarah could see everyone's disappointment in the slumps of their shoulders.

"Come on, guys," she said. "We have some ice cream to scoop!"

Lizzie gave a small smile, and Olive nodded. They all walked out to the front of the stand.

Hakeem stood first in line, holding on to a copy of the *Daily News*. He said to Lizzie with a big grin, "I'll have the 'Ice Cream Summers Make the Best Friends' sundae." He added, "I know Camila would have really liked this one."

Lizzie said, "Huh?"

"The 'Ice Cream Summers Make the Best Friends' sundae, please," Hakeem repeated, still beaming. He pointed to the paper. "I read about this fabulous creation in this paper."

More and more people—mostly adults—had started lining up behind him. Including Sarah's mom and Mr. and Ms. Garrison and Olive and Peter's dads. Sarah stared in astonishment at the line, which had started snaking down the road. She hadn't even known this many people lived in New Amity!

Peter said, eyeing the line, "We haven't really put it up for sale. We don't have a price for it."

"Hmm. I tell you what. Why don't you let everyone pay you what they want for it? You'd be surprised what people will pay for great creations." Hakeem smiled more. "Though, now that I think about it, that might be too much for me, the sundae. How about a vanilla cone?"

Peter looked at Olive, who looked at Sarah, who looked at Lizzie. Sarah shrugged. Lizzie scooped the vanilla ice cream and put it on the cone that Sarah had grabbed. She passed it to Olive, who gave it to Peter to ring up.

"Uh, that'll be a dollar twenty-five," he said.

Hakeem chuckled. "Oh, no. I'll pay what I would have paid for the sundae. Here's fifty dollars. It's worth every penny." He handed Peter a fifty-dollar bill, took his cone, and walked away, smiling. Peter held on to the money and stared at the other three, looking as confused as Sarah felt.

Aaron and Rachel were next. "Yes, we'll have two 'Ice Cream Summers Make the Best Friends.' Only make one a chocolate-dipped cone and the other a Neapolitan cone, will you?" Aaron said. Lizzie and Sarah made the order, Olive gave it to them, and Peter rang them up.

Rachel added, "We think this sundae sounds like the best thing ever. We're really proud of all of you." They left a hundred dollars on the counter, smiled at the four friends, then walked away.

Beckett was next, and Sarah saw her mom beaming behind him. "Hey, guys," Beckett said. "Ms. Shirvani here told me about your entry in the contest. So I wrote about it in the paper. Kids working at the coolest ice cream stand making the coolest ice cream sundae? Now that's interesting. Especially the part where you're trying to get a zombie hayride going. It's too bad you didn't win that contest." He looked back at the line and smiled. "But it looks like that zombie hayride might happen anyway. Oh, and I want a triple fudge sundae."

Sarah's mouth fell open. She'd just noticed: every single adult in line had a copy of the paper. And every single one was smiling at them.

For the next hour, Sarah, Lizzie, Peter, and Olive ran around, getting people ice cream and watching as their fund for the zombie hayride grew. They helped Ms. Henderson and Stella, Noa from the grocery store, Mariko and Aldo, Sveta and Dani, and of course, Sheriff Hadley. He left three hundred dollars on the counter, and he winked at Sarah and tipped his hat. Sarah grinned so big, it almost hurt.

Lizzie's parents chipped in, Sarah's mom, Peter and Olive's dads . . . even Gloria gave them some of her babysitting money. She pulled down her sunglasses and looked over them at the four. "You're lucky today I'm practicing being Mother Teresa for a play." She winked and then yelled "ACTING!" as she walked away.

After another hour of people asking for ice cream, the stand finally cleared out. Sarah's heart was so full, it felt like it could burst. She knew how her mom felt now about that commercial.

Peter counted the money while Sarah, Lizzie, and Olive waited impatiently. Or at least Sarah was impatient. She shifted from foot to foot until Lizzie gave her a look.

Finally, Peter looked up, his eyes wide. "Uh, this is six thousand dollars right here."

For the second time that day, Sarah's mouth flew open. That was one thousand dollars OVER what they needed for the hayride.

"You guys . . . ," she said at the same time that Olive said, "Whoa," and Lizzie squeaked.

Peter smiled. "I think it's safe to say this fall we'll be able to make a zombie hayride."

"WOOO-HOOOO!" Sarah shouted, and jumped in the air. All of them grabbed each other and hugged and, if Sarah was honest, maybe even cried a little.

"We couldn't have done this without you," she said to Olive and Peter.

Olive shook her head. "Thanks for letting us help with the stand. We're lucky to have you as friends!"

Lizzie said, "We're the lucky ones!"

Peter shook his head. "No, we definitely are."

"I swear I will beat you all up if you don't get that we're the lucky ones!" Sarah pretend-glared at them and they pretend-glared back. Then they dissolved in giggles. She looked at them and felt warm all the way through. Then she straightened up. "But enough goofing around. We need to put our heads together and figure out how to go about this zombie hayride!"

The four of them took off their aprons, talking excitedly about ideas for the fall.

As they left, Sarah took a look at the stand that had brought everyone together. She had been right. This really was the best. Summer. Ever.

ACKNOWLEDGMENTS

No book is written in a vacuum, and this one certainly is no exception.

I want to thank my amazing agent, Ammi-Joan Paquette, first and foremost for getting me this opportunity and for being LITERALLY and LITERARILY the best agent ever. Joan—you are so truly awesome.

A HUGE thank-you to my editor, Emma Sector, for her patience, insight, and enthusiasm throughout this whole writing process. Seriously—you all want Emma as your editor if you write anything at all. But she has to help me with the next three books first, so wait just a bit?

ACKNOWLEDGMENTS

I can't thank Anne Ursu enough for her unending support and for her unthanked and unpaid job of talking me down and talking me through everything writing related. And . . . well, let's be real: everything. Did you know she is an actual angel? It's true. A big thank-you to Sharon Kahnke, Shaun Murphy, Megan Vossler, Brett Kallusky, Jordan Brown, Natalie Harter, Patrick Jones, Jenny Halstead, Pete Webster, and many others—like Christine Heppermann and Laura Ruby!—who have been sources of constant support and awesomeness for years and years and years. See? It was all worth it! You're in a book! Some of you have written books already, so this might not be as big a draw as I'm hoping. . . . Ahem. Anyway. Thank you, my loves.

By that same token, I want to mention Ella Kahnke as a fan who has kept me writing for so many years now. Thank you, Ella! I can't wait until I get to read your books in the years to come!

Finally, always and forever, a thank-you to my family. From extended family like my awesome sister-cousin, Melanie, to immediate family like my brother, Scott, and sister-in-law, Marlie. And my AWESOME, GORGEOUS perfect nieces, Bri and Colette. And to my mom and dad, who have always supported me in ways huge, big, medium, and small. I love you all so much.

MEGAN ATWOOD is a writer, editor, and professor in Minneapolis whose most recent books include the Dear Molly, Dear Olive series. When she's not writing books for kids of all ages, she's making new friends, going on zombie hayrides, and eating as much ice cream as she can. And, always, petting her two adorable cats, who "help" her write every book.

Don't miss Book 2:

ONCE UPON A WINTER

It's winter in the orchard, and Peter is fed up.
No one listens to him, and it's so very cold! Then
he thinks he's discovered a magical portal to
another world. Will that make everything better?